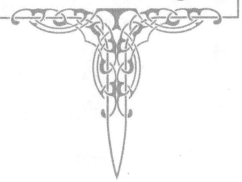

draven's light

TALES OF GOLDSTONE WOOD

NOVELLAS OF GOLDSTONE WOOD

draven's light

TALES OF GOLDSTONE WOOD

—•◄✦►•—

ANNE ELISABETH STENGL

ROOGLEWOOD PRESS

Raleigh, NC

Published by Rooglewood Press

www.RooglewoodPress.com

Printed in the United States of America

ISBN-13: 978-1-942379-02-7

This is a work of fiction. Names, characters, incidents, and dialogues are products of the author's imagination and are not to be construed as real. Any resemblance to actual events or persons, living or dead, is entirely coincidental.

Book design by A.E. de Silva

Cover art by Mihaela Voicu

Stock image "Nordic Warrior" by Lia Konrad

To Beka,
for the beginning.

To Handsome,
for the end.

THE HIGH PROMONTORY

ACH STEP DRAGGING more than the last, the girl climbed the winding track up the hill. She progressed so slowly, with such hesitation, that one might have thought she bore a terrible weight. But no; her arms clutched the waterskin to her thin breast without apparent strain. She had carried far heavier burdens often enough in her short life. Nevertheless, her pace dragged, and her gaze, darting up the path and down again to stare at her feet, was filled with apprehension.

"I need you to make the run for me today," her mother had told her but a short while ago. "I have no time, and it is the least we owe them. Hurry, child."

"Cannot Grandmother go with me?" the girl had protested, her eyes rounding even as her mother placed the waterskin in her hands. The outer hide was slippery, and the girl was obliged to hold it close so as not to drop it.

"Certainly not!" her mother had replied. "You hurry along now, and don't be bothering your grandmother. She needs her rest and can't spend her days holding your hand anymore."

But the girl hadn't moved. She had stood quite still, the waterskin dampening the front of her rough-fibered gown, staring up at her mother. Then, very softly, she said, "I'm afraid."

But her mother had no patience. "Afraid of what?" she had cried and, without waiting for an answer, turned her daughter around and gave her a firm push toward the hill-winding track. "Don't be a coward. Go on! It's wrong to keep those poor men waiting all day. I can't be expected to run every errand, and you are quite a big girl now."

She didn't feel quite a big girl. She felt small. She always felt small when she walked this track, but never so small as she did now, climbing it alone for the first time. Always before she had gone in company with someone: her father, sometimes her busy mother, even one of her aunts or older cousins. Always before she had held onto someone's hand and gathered courage from a stronger grasp.

But not today. Today she must face the enormity of the Great House on her own. The Great House . . . and the Brothers who built it.

As long as the girl could remember, the Brothers had worked on the top of the hill, going about their endless labor. As long as she could remember, she had watched from Kallias Village down below as, day by day, month by month, year by year, the great walls had risen up from the tree line to tower on that promontory above the river. In winter the labor ceased for a time, and the Brothers went away to far-off quarries (or so her father told her), there to mine and shape enormous blocks of stone.

But as soon as the binding of winter gave way to the freedom of spring, the Brothers would return, accompanied by strange, fierce folk and stranger, fiercer animals, hauling the new stone up the track—which was quite wide by now after many years of this cyclical process—up to the very top of the hill. The strange folk and the fierce animals always left soon after, never speaking to the men or woman of the village.

But the Brothers remained. And throughout the rest of the year the ringing song of hammers upon stone echoed down from the promontory, as much a part of each day's music as birdsong or the voice of the river itself.

The girl heard the hammer song now—*Clang! Clang! Clang!* Only one hammer singing a lonely melody, she thought. Slow and rhythmic, without haste but with great patience. She matched her stride to that beat.

Clang! Clang! Clang!

Step. Step. Step.

Though her pace was reluctant, her heart beat like mad in her breast. She could feel it thudding against the waterskin. Would the Brothers speak to her? They never had before, though the Kind One had smiled at her upon occasion. His was a nice smile . . . but still! She dreaded the very thought of his speaking and, worse still, expecting her to answer.

The walk up the hill was a long one, but the late-spring day was fair, and the girl's going, slow. She should not have felt so winded. But as the trees gave way at last to the large clear space at the crown of the hill and she looked out upon the rising stone walls of the Great House, she gasped and could hardly catch her breath.

To compare the Great House to even the largest structures of Kallias Village would be like comparing the wingspan of the northern eagles to that of the little chaffinches living down in the brier. The difference was so vast that no comparison could be justly made! The Great House, even unfinished as it was, could have held all of Kallias in its main hall and many of the fields surrounding in its courtyard. The doors themselves, newly carved and hung by the hand of the Kind One, were each as large as the entire floor space of her father's house. The stones comprising the walls—so carefully cut in those fabled, far-off quarries and shaped upon arrival to fit seamlessly one against another— were shot with blue and gold, unlike any mined in any quarry within a hundred miles, perhaps within a thousand. Indeed, these stones were so otherworldly in their beauty, they did not seem as though they could come from this world at all. The gold in them caught the light of the sun and held it, warm and glowing and alive.

But while this was enough to overwhelm the girl, it was not enough to make her afraid. No, she trembled because, through the open door, she could see inside the hall. And it was dark. Dark like the fall of night. Dark like the mouth of a yawning mine. Dark like the beginning and the end of the world. Though the walls were lined with tall windows and the roof above was as yet incomplete, its rafters etched against the sky like the ribcage of some giant beast, no light seemed able to penetrate down into the shadows cast within.

So the girl stood on the edge of the tree line, staring up at the Great House and unable to make her feet move. She saw, high above on a wooden scaffolding, a tiny figure moving. The figure was tiny only for distance, and even at that distance she knew the form at once for one of the Brothers. The Strong One, as she always thought of him.

The singing of the hammer stopped. The figure of the Strong One stood and stretched. She knew that he had seen her, and she knew that she must proceed. They were expecting her, after all.

She approached, each step a battle of wills with her own fearful heart. She watched as the Strong One began to descend the scaffolding. Soon she was near enough to the House and he close enough to the ground that she could see the dust of carving on his face, streaked with lines of sweat. But it was hard to notice such things when near to either of the Brothers. For no matter how covered with the dust of this world they became, no amount of dirt could disguise the overwhelming, shining beauty of either of them.

The girl felt her throat thicken with terror as the Strong One leapt down the last scaffold ladder and strode toward her. The sun was on his hair, making it shine like pure gold, and his eyes were like the sky above, only brighter and full of the hammer's song. A song of strength and metal and rock. A song that could echo across a nation.

"Well met, little one," the Strong One said as he approached, and he smiled. But his smile was nothing like the smile of the Kind One. The girl couldn't bear to look at it. "Are you come alone today?"

She nodded, fixing her gaze upon the ground at his feet, and offered up the waterskin. She continued to stare at the same spot while the Strong One took the water and drank deeply. This was the only price the Brothers asked for the work they did on the promontory: water from the river sent up once a day. And when the water came, both drank and both seemed satisfied. It was uncanny. No other men the girl knew could work such long, such difficult hours, morning, noon, and night, with only a single draught of water to refresh them each day. This was one of a hundred different reasons she knew the Brothers were not like normal men.

Indeed, they might not be men at all.

She studied the ground beneath the Strong One's feet until she could have told from memory the arrangement of each stone fleck fallen down from the hammering work performed high above. She could have told how the thin stalk of grass bent under the pressure of the Strong One's boot, the tiny golden flower at its end bowed down and touching the dirt.

"Thank you, child," said the Strong One, having finished his drink.

He knelt, his head drawing level with hers. She turned her chin slightly to one side the better to avoid meeting his otherworldly gaze. "You are kind to bring us water all the way up from the village. It is a long walk for a small girl. Are you tired?"

She shook her head once and quickly.

He nodded and rubbed the stubble on his chin with a dust-grimed hand, saying nothing. There was an awkwardness about his silence, as though he sought for a certain word but couldn't find it. It made the girl even more uncomfortable, and she wished he would rise and climb back up his high scaffold, freeing her from his studying eyes.

"Lumé," he sighed at last, straightening up to his full, towering height. "I fear I'm not graced with gentle words for children. You should run along, find Akilun inside. He has the right way about him." Then, as though as eager to be free of her as she was to be free of him, the Strong One turned and started toward the scaffold.

But he had only just grasped the ladder when the girl, suddenly finding her voice, gasped, "Inside?"

The Strong One turned and looked over his shoulder, his face wearing a puzzled frown. "Yes," he said. "Inside. Go on then. Hopefully he won't scare you as I seem to!" With a self-deprecating grin, he hastened on up the ladder, leaving the girl standing in the scaffold's shadow.

The girl looked down and found that the waterskin was back in her hands, though she did not remember taking it from the Strong One. She stared at it as though somehow it might offer some solution to this newest problem, this newest terror.

But there was no solution. She must enter the shadows of the hall. She must step into the Great House.

Perhaps she could run. Perhaps she could turn now and flee back down the track, emptying the skin in the dirt as she went. Her mother would never know; she wouldn't even ask. No one would ever have to know.

Except . . . except the Kind One. He would know. For he wouldn't receive his daily gift of water. And he would wonder why, when he asked so little, even that was denied him.

She found that she was staring at that bent stalk and the gold blossom. The stalk was slowly rising back into an upright stance, the little flower bravely raising its bright face to the world. As it lifted, so the girl felt her quailing heart lift in her breast. She would enter the House. She would deliver the gift.

So on trembling legs the girl crossed the dust-shrouded yard, stepping around piles of discarded stone, avoiding sharp tools of some metal far stronger than she had ever before seen—stronger even than the bronze tools with which her father and his men worked the land around Kallias—and made her way to the great doors. These had been carved and hung when the girl's mother was still a child. But the girl had never seen them up close.

She approached them now with equal parts trepidation and curiosity, staring at the doors themselves so that she would not have to look at the darkness beyond them. The doors were fascinating to behold anyway, for the enormous panels of wood had been so carefully carved, smoothed, and treated that they scarcely looked like wood anymore. Indeed, they were the soft hides of stags and does, the powerful pinions of eagles' wings, the pounding hooves of mighty horses, the shining of a sky full of stars.

So gifted was the Kind One's hand that he could make these things, and more, come alive in the planed heartwood of a tree. The girl stared open-mouthed, seeing the doors truly for the first time. And she realized, the closer she came, that her first impressions had been wrong. Or, if not wholly wrong, then not wholly true either. For what she had taken to be stags and does were indeed more like men with antlers sprouting from their brows, and women with the haunches of deer and soft, up-pricked doe's ears. What she had believed were eagles' wings actually belonged to great cat-headed beasts with thick manes about their necks. Other wings sprouted from horses' shoulders, bearing them up into the star-filled skies among the wood-carven clouds.

The girl stood in the very shadows of the door, staring at the panels and the many carvings. Those visions she beheld were far beyond her comprehension, and she felt her brain growing numb. Indeed, when she blinked it seemed to her that all the fantastic figures melted away and became once more beings she could understand: deer, eagles, horses.

"Who is there, please?"

The girl startled at the voice coming from just beyond the door. She forgot her awe at the carvings, and all her fear returned. She opened her mouth to answer but could find no words. Thus she stood dumb and ashamed as one of the two doors creaked heavily on its hinges, allowing space for the second of the two Brothers to look through.

The Kind One, seeing the child standing shivering on the step, smiled gently. The girl felt her heart melt inside her along with some of her fear. His was such a lovely smile!

"Good morrow, child," said the Kind One, looking down upon her and taking in the waterskin clutched to her chest. "I've met you before, haven't I? You are Iulia's daughter, I think."

The girl nodded.

"Is your mother not with you today?"

The girl shook her head. Then, without a word, she held out the waterskin. Still smiling, the Kind One accepted it and drank, even as his brother had. When he had finished, he emptied the last drops in his hands and washed them. Only then did he address the girl again. "It is good you came when you did," he said. "I am just beginning an important work, and it is wise to pursue such tasks with clean hands."

She felt she was meant to say something. Perhaps to ask a question, to inquire as to what this work might be. But she could only stare, and even that took more courage than she liked to admit.

"I believe I know your name," said the Kind One, considering her. He spoke her name then and asked, "Am I right?"

"Yes," the girl whispered.

"It is a good name. A very good name." He handed the waterskin back to her but hesitated, even as his brother had before returning to his work. Unlike the Strong One, he was confident in his way with children, and his confidence gave the girl heart. "Would you like to see what I am working on?" he asked.

Much to the girl's surprise, she nodded.

"All right. Come on then."

He put out his hand, and she took it without a thought. Something about holding the hand of someone so much bigger, older, and stronger than she made her feel better than she had since she began this long trek. Tucking the now-empty waterskin under her other arm, she allowed herself to be led through the great doors, even into the shadows of the hall. Now that the Kind One held her fast, she found she wasn't so frightened as she might have been.

And truly, once she was through the doors the shadows were not as deep as she had thought. Long spears of sunlight fell across the floor and up along the opposite wall, and she could see many details of the hall's interior, details she had never imagined. For the carving on the doors was not the only evidence of the Kind One's handiwork. The walls were brilliant with murals worked in multi-colored flecks of stone. The supporting beams were carved in fantastical patterns, many in a sun-and-moon motif, others in designs she could not name. The floor at her feet displayed a wonderful image of the sun worked in color-treated wood, highly polished so as to shine where the light struck it. She glimpsed statues shaped like angels and other more fantastical beings. She glimpsed tapestries woven and embroidered by the hands of Faerie maids.

On the opposite end of the hall was another set of doors facing east. These were closed fast. They looked so very heavy, the girl wondered if it were possible for a single man to open them.

The girl could have stood in one place and stared about her for hours. But the Kind One led her across the hall—led her for what seemed like miles, so vast was the interior—to a place along the northern wall. There a small gleaming lantern burned bright, illuminating a tool-littered workspace. Bathed in the lantern's light stood an ugly, fat stump. It was all that remained of quite a large tree, the branches long ago cleft from the trunk, the bark peeled away to reveal the wood beneath. It stood six feet tall and more, taller than the Strong One, even.

The girl found her footsteps slowing as the Kind One led her toward that stump. She stopped while still many paces from it and refused to go nearer, so that he was obliged to let go of her hand. Though she couldn't have told why if asked, she knew that she did not like that stump. There was something . . . something *wrong* about it. Something even the light of the lantern could not heal.

The Kind One, letting her stand where she stopped, approached the lantern. "I have only just made a start,' he said, "but you might find it interesting." He bent and picked up the lantern by its handle, lifting it up and shining its light more clearly on the stump's surface.

The girl gasped. There was a face in the wood.

Among her tribe there were many who carved and made little trinkets out of wood or bronze or clay. And, of course, she had so recently seen and admired other lovely carvings done by the Kind One's gifted hand. But never before had she seen a face rendered so lifelike in wood-caught immobility. She stared at it, wonder-struck, and forgot her dislike of the stump itself. Without realizing she did so, she drew closer, stepping into the lantern-glow. The light filled her eyes so that they shone with an understanding beyond rational thought.

She turned to the Kind One, and she wasn't afraid of him when she asked, "Who is that?"

"He was called Draven," said the Kind One. "He was a man I knew. Long ago by the years as counted in your world. But it seems only yesterday to me."

"I don't know him," said the girl. "I don't know his name."

"You know him by another name," said the Kind One. "He had three names in his lifetime. I knew him as Draven."

"When did you meet him?" asked the girl, turning from the Kind One to study the face above her once more. He seemed young to her. An adult, certainly, but not an old one. Not so old as her father, for sure, nor her mother. Definitely not so old as either of the Brothers, though they had a way about them that seemed both youthful and ancient at the same time. She thought the face in the wood oddly familiar, though she couldn't say why. "Was he a man of Kallias?"

"No," said the Kind One. "He was not. He was born of the tribe across the river."

"There is no tribe across the river," said the girl.

"Not anymore. But there used to be."

"What happened to them?"

The Kind One, still holding his lantern high, smiled a mysterious sort of smile that held many secrets. "It is a long story," he said. "I doubt that I can tell it all in one afternoon, not with the work I have ahead of me. But I'll make you a pact, Iulia's daughter: If you will agree to return with water for me tomorrow and for the several days following, I will do what I can to spin out this tale for you. What do you say?"

All fear forgotten, at least for the moment, the girl sat down before the ugly stump and the young face carved in wood. She sat in the light of the silver lantern, her elbows on her knees, her chin in her hand. As the Kind One took up his hammer and chisel and began, ever so carefully, to chip away at the old wood, she listened to what he said. He began in the traditional manner of all great tale-spinners:

"Let me tell you a story."

THE NAME
OF A MAN

HE HEARD THE DRUMS in his dreams, distant but drawing ever nearer. He had heard them before and wondered if the time of his manhood had come. But with the approach of dawn, the drums always faded away and he woke to the world still a child. Still a boy.

But this night, the distant drums were louder, stronger. Somehow he knew they were not concocted of his sleeping fancy. No, even as he slept he knew these were real drums, and he recognized the beat: The beat of death. The beat of blood.

The beat of a man's heart.

He woke with a start, his leg throbbing where it had just been kicked. It was not the sort of awakening he had longed for these last two years and more. He glared from his bed up into the face of his sister, who stood above him, balancing her weight on a stout forked branch tucked under her left shoulder.

"Ita," the boy growled, "what are you doing here? Go back to the women's hut!"

His sister made a face at him, but he saw, even by the moonlight streaming through cracks in the thatch above, that her eyes were very round and solemn. Only then did he notice that the drumbeats of his dream were indeed still booming deep in the woods beyond the village fires. He sat up then, his heart thudding its own thunderous pace.

"A prisoner," Ita said, shifting her branch so that she might turn toward the door. "The drums speak of a prisoner. They're bringing him even now." She flashed a smile down at him, though it was so tense with anxiety it could hardly be counted a smile at all. "Gaho, your name!"

The boy was up and out of his bed in a moment, reaching for a tunic and belt. His sister hobbled back along the wall but did not leave, though he wished she would. He wished she would allow him these few moments before the drums arrived in the village. The drums that beat of one man's death . . . and one man's birth.

His name was Gaho. But by the coming of dawn, if the drums' promise were true, he would be born again in blood and bear a new name.

Hands shaking with what he desperately hoped wasn't fear, he tightened his belt and searched the room for his sickle blade. He saw the bone handle, white in the moonlight, protruding from beneath his bed pile, and swiftly took it up. The bronze gleamed dully, like the carnivorous tooth of an ancient beast.

A shudder ran through his sister's body. Gaho, sensing her distress, turned to her. She grasped her supporting branch hard, and the smile was gone from her face. "Gaho," she said, "will you do it?"

"I will," said Gaho, his voice strong with mounting excitement.

But Ita reached out to him suddenly, catching his weapon hand just above the wrist. "I will lose you," she said. "My brother . . . I will lose you!"

"You will not. You will lose only Gaho," said the boy, shaking her off, gently, for she was not strong. Without another word, he ducked through the door of his small sod house—one he had built for himself but a year before in anticipation of his coming manhood—and stood in the darkness of Rannul Village, eyes instinctively turning to the few campfires burning. The drums were very near now, and he could see the shadows of waking villagers moving about the fires, building up the flames in preparation for what must surely follow. He felt eyes he could not see turning to his house, turning to him. He felt the question each pair of eyes asked in silent curiosity: *Will it be tonight?*

Tonight or no night.

Grasping the hilt of his weapon with both hands, Gaho strode to the dusty village center, which was beaten down into hard, packed earth from years of meetings and matches of strength held in this same spot. Tall pillars of aged wood ringed this circle, and women hastened to these, bearing torches which they fit into hollowed-out slots in each pillar. Soon the village center was bright as noonday, but with harsh red light appropriate for coming events.

Gaho stood in the center of that light, his heart ramming in his throat though his face was a stoic mask. All the waking village were gathered now, men, women, and children, standing just beyond the circle, watching him.

And the drums came up from the river, pounding in time to the tramp of warriors' feet. Then the warriors themselves were illuminated by the ringing torches, their faces anointed in blood, their heads helmed with bone and bronze, their shoulders covered in hides of bear, wolf, and boar. Ten men carried tight skin drums, beating them with their fists. They entered the center first, standing each beneath one of the ringing pillars. Other warriors followed them, filling in the gaps between.

Then the chieftain, mighty Gaher, appeared. He carried his heavy crescent ax in one hand, and Gaho saw that blood stained its edge—indeed, blood spattered the blade from tip to hilt and covered the whole of the chieftain's fist. Gaher strode into the circle, and the boy saw more blood in his beard. But he also saw the bright, wolfish smile, and knew for certain that his sister had been correct. The night of naming had come.

"My son," said the chief, saluting Gaho with upraised weapon.

"My father," said Gaho, raising his sickle blade in return.

"Are you ready this night to die and live again?" asked the chief. His voice carried through the shadows, and every one of the tribe heard it, as did any and all listening beasts of forest and field surrounding. "Are you ready this night for the spilling of blood that must flow before life may begin?"

Gaho drew a deep breath, putting all the strength of his spirit into his answer. "I am ready, Father."

Gaher's smile grew, the torchlight flashing upon his sharpened canines. He turned then and motioned to the darkness beyond the torchlight.

And the sacrifice was brought forward.

At first Gaho could discern little of the man who staggered between two warriors as they dragged him. The rush and roar in his ears was such that it drowned out all other perception. But he shook himself and focused his energies. Indeed, he must be as focused as the razor edge of his blade. He forced himself to take in what he could of this man who would provide his due bloodletting.

The man wore a sack over his head, but the rest of him was stripped down to nothing but his rough-woven trousers. Even the leg-wraps had been removed, leaving the loose trousers to billow about his calves like a child's garments. His chest was bare, and Gaho saw the bleeding wound in his shoulder. Already the bloodletting had begun.

Who is he? Gaho wanted to ask. But perhaps it was better not to know. He was not a man of Rannul, and that alone mattered. No man of Rannul would kill one of his own, not even for so important a ceremony. He had probably been fetched from over the river, some farmer caught sleeping too far from the safety of his village's fires and the protection of his chieftain's warriors.

Gaho squared his shoulders even as the prisoner was dragged before him and forced to his knees. Chief Gaher stood at Gaho's side and indicated the prisoner with a wave of his hand. "Will you slay him thus?"

Gaho considered for only a breath. It would be a worthy bloodletting, but he did not feel it right to take his man's name so easily. He shook his head. "I will not. I will fight," he said.

Gaher nodded his satisfaction at his son's answer. He had likely dealt the prisoner's wound himself, making certain he was disabled. No reason to risk the life of a chieftain's son. But a fight was still good, a noble answer.

So, at a word from their chief, the warriors holding the prisoner stripped away the sack over his head. Gaho looked into the face of the man he would kill.

His heart stopped. He had not expected the prisoner to be so young. Near his own age, in fact, perhaps a little older. A fierce terror darted from the young man's eyes, and he stared up at Gaho as though gazing upon the blackest of all devils. There was a gag in his mouth, and he strained against it like a dog worrying a muzzle. One of the warriors slipped a knife up alongside the prisoner's head and cut the gag loose.

The prisoner gasped, jerking away from the knife. But he rallied himself, drawing a deep breath and holding his torso upright even as he knelt before his enemies. "Unbind me and set me free!" he cried, his voice thick with an accent that confirmed he came from over the river.

"We will unbind you, certainly," said Gaher, motioning again to his warriors. They hesitated, but only briefly, before cutting the ropes securing the prisoner's arms. Immediately the prisoner leapt to his feet, turning this way and that. But he was ringed by his enemies, all of them armed and deadly. There was no use in running.

The prisoner turned back to Gaher, his jaw tightly clenched. Then he said, "My father will not stand for this. It will mean war between Kahorn and Rannul. They will set upon you with fury, demanding the life of every man and boy. Your women will weep with the desolation of widowhood and bereavement, crying out for their own deaths!"

Gaho knew then who stood before him. This was no farmer. This was Callix, son of Callor, prince of the Kahorn tribe.

How far had his father's men penetrated into the territory across the river to gain such a prize? It did not seem possible, for the nearest Kahorn village was a day's march at least beyond the banks of River Hanna. Could it be that this prince of Kahorn had wandered into Rannul territory? A fortunate chance! Not one to be missed.

But Gaho felt his gut sickening.

"Men of Kahorn will be upon your shores before sunset three days hence!" the prisoner-prince declared, gesticulating wildly with his right arm. His left hung limp at his side, blood from the shoulder wound dripping down in slow stain. But he glared at Gaher with princely fervor. "You bring war upon your people."

Gaher stepped forward, drawing a knife from his belt. This he tossed to the dirt at the prisoner's feet even as he leaned in to growl in his face: "Good."

With that, he turned his back upon the prisoner and strode to the edge of the village center. His warriors backed away as well, leaving Gaho alone in the middle of the torchlight, facing the Prince of Kahorn, who panted and stared around him in disbelieving horror. At last the prisoner's staring eyes fell upon Gaho.

Gaho, who was taller already than most men in Rannul. Gaho, who, though he bore a boy's name, boasted the breadth and strength of a bear. Gaho, proud son of Gaher, a fellow prince. A deadly enemy.

Gaho gazed down at his victim, who was half a head shorter than he. He indicated the knife at his feet. "Arm yourself and prepare for death," he said.

The prisoner, who had been pale before, now looked sickly grey. Not even the torchlight could warm his skin. He stooped, however, and took up the blade. "Is this how warriors of Rannul get their sport?" he demanded through white lips. "Hewing at wounded men?"

Gaho took a step forward then paused. He glanced first at the bronze blade in the prisoner's hand, then at the great extent of his own sickle sword. He had chosen to fight, to let blood in combat and thus achieve his manhood. But with such a disparity of weapons and strength, could he truly claim manhood following such a bloodletting?

The women of Rannul gasped as Gaho tossed his blade to land in the dirt behind him. The warriors on the border of the village center tightened their grips on their own weapons. But Gaher only smiled even as his son, unarmed, began to approach the prisoner.

The Kahorn prince's gaze darted to the discarded sickle blade then back to Gaho's face. If anything, his fear redoubled. What sort of foe was this, who did not fear to go unarmed into combat? The prisoner clutched the blade in his good hand and, moving in a half-crouch, circled round, trying to discover an opening for a lunge. Gaho, though beardless, had the look of a warrior, and the prisoner had seen enough of war, even in his short years, to know better than to let his guard drop.

Suddenly the prisoner attacked, his blade upraised and slashing. If he had not been weak from blood loss, he may have met his mark. But Gaho, moving with surprising speed despite his bulk, twisted to one side and brought both fists down together between the prisoner's shoulders. The breath knocked from his body, the prisoner landed in the dust at Gaho's feet. Struggling to draw air into his lungs, he rolled to one side, lashing out at Gaho's leg with the knife.

Gaho, however, leapt back and, with a single kick, sent the knife flying through the air to land well out of the prisoner's reach. He flung himself upon the prisoner, his fists striking at his face and chest. The prisoner raised his good arm in defense and managed to land a kick in Gaho's stomach.

Gaho staggered back, clutching his gut, and his eyes flashed. The heat of bloodlust began to take hold, roaring in his veins. He saw not the living prisoner but the dead sacrifice that must be made before the light of dawn.

With a roar that was scarcely human he lunged at the prisoner, who was getting to his feet. The prisoner avoided Gaho's clutching arms, but only just, and one fist caught him in the side. He staggered and went down on one knee then used the momentum of his fall to avoid yet another swinging blow. Gaho kicked him, sending him sprawling.

The prisoner writhed, desperate to turn himself around to face his enemy. But Gaho was atop him, pressing him facedown into the dirt. The prisoner's fear-filled eyes lit upon the dagger only a few handbreadths beyond his reach. He kicked and flailed, succeeding in landing a blow on Gaho's arm.

Gaho did not know himself anymore. He knew only the surging in his heart, the pound of blood in his ears as forceful as any drumbeat. He could feel his adulthood, so very near now, just on the edge of his grasp. He would be a warrior. He would forgo the name of a child and take up his man's name, standing at the right hand of his mighty father. After this, his first blood, he would march into battle and take the lives of many warriors, thus proving his strength and his courage again and again.

Only one thing stood in the way of this dream and its fulfillment. Only this prisoner scrabbling in the dust, his life a thin thread strained to the breaking point. One swift slice and . . .

Gaho drove his knee into the prisoner's wounded shoulder. The prisoner gave a thin cry, and for an instant ceased to struggle. Then his efforts redoubled, his good arm stretching to its full extent, striving for the dagger that lay now only a finger's width away. Leaning across his prey, Gaho plucked up the dagger. He could have slit the prisoner's throat then, but that did not seem to him the right way to usher in his manhood. He preferred to look into his enemy's eyes.

He lifted his weight from the prisoner's shoulder, standing back to allow the prisoner to scramble free and upright. Panting heavily, almost spent, the prisoner got to his feet and faced Gaho. His limbs shuddered, and his face was streaked with dirt and sweat and blood. Everything about his stance bespoke defeat. Everything except his eyes, which flashed with a prince's pride.

"Go on, then!" he growled, beckoning Gaho with his good hand. "Try your hand. I'm almost bled out! See what short work you can make of me."

Gaho took one step, and another. His arm was even now upraised, ready to plunge the knife to its mark.

Suddenly a pale white face seemed to swim before his eyes.

As though in a dream, he thought the face stood between him and his enemy. But no. No, she stood beyond him, just within the torchlight, a few paces apart from other villagers. Ita, his sister, looked on with wide eyes, leaning on her supporting branch.

And her eyes seemed to say to him, even as she had said but a short while before: *I will lose you.*

Already Gaho was taking his third step. With the fourth, he reached out with his empty fist and caught the prisoner by the throat, throwing him to the ground. He pressed his knee into his enemy's chest, the knife upraised. He looked into the eyes of his sacrifice.

But he saw his sister's eyes instead.

I will lose you.

The roaring in his ears was almost more than a man could bear. Far more than a boy could withstand. He must give in. He must deal the blow, spill the blood. He must earn his name.

The prisoner, all fear lost in rage, snarled up at him, too weak to move. Too weak to defend himself.

Gaho felt his chest heaving, his heart ramming against his ribcage. It seemed to him that he felt these things from a distance, as though they were happening to someone else. Even the berserker thunder in his head no longer belonged to him. He stood upon the outside.

And he asked himself, *Is this who you will be?*

In that moment he knew something he would never have dared to face or admit. Something no boy of Rannul would acknowledge without the deepest, most searing burn of shame. But he knew the truth, and there was no point in denying it. Even as the bloodlust cleared from his head and the light of death faded from his eyes, he accepted the bitter truth in his heart: He was no killer.

Shame fell heavily upon his shoulders. Later he had no memory of his next several actions. He could not remember dropping the knife. He could not remember rising up and backing away from the prisoner, who lay panting but otherwise unmoving in the dirt. He never could recall how he turned and approached his father, bowing deeply.

Afterward he was told that his words were "It is done." But he had no memory of speaking them.

Gaher gazed down upon his son. His own face was now as pale as death, and the lines of his mouth were merciless and hard. And disbelieving. He tried a few times to speak before he found his voice. Never before had any man of Rannul heard his chieftain's voice tremble. But it trembled now as he said, "Your man's name, my son. Is this how you would achieve it?"

For all had seen the match. All had seen the strength of Gaher's son. All had seen him bring his enemy down, like a dog pulling a hart from its flying feet. All had seen what should have been.

And yet the prisoner lived.

"Is this how you would end your bloodletting? Even now, as first light approaches?" Gaher demanded.

Dawn touched the rim of the world, and the sun rose slowly, his golden eye peering down upon the shame displayed below. There were no clouds to mar his view, no coverings for the chieftain and his son.

Gaho nodded and did not meet his father's gaze. "It is done," he said. "I am no longer a boy."

"And you are no true man," said Gaher. "Nor are you any son of mine. I give you one last chance. Slay your enemy, or you will never bear the name intended for you. Do you understand me?"

"I understand," whispered his son.

"And you will not obey?"

The boy who was now a man bowed beneath the weight of his chieftain's displeasure. But he said only, "It is done."

Gaher's lips drew back in an animal snarl. The warriors surrounding saw his hand move to his ax and wondered if he would slay his son. But instead, clenching both hands into fists, Gaher took a step back. His voice was full of wrath as he spoke, but it was clear and even.

"Very well. You have achieved your manhood. But no true man and no true son are you. I will not name you Gaheris. You are instead Draven,

Fainthearted. This is your doom, brought down upon your own head."

So Gaho died that dawn. In his place beneath the rising sun stood Draven the Coward.

ACROSS THE RIVER

THE GIRL SAT with her chin cradled in her hands, gazing up at the face wrought in wood above her. The Kind One worked while he told his tale, and during the telling the face had taken on still more definition. Long hair curled around the square cheeks and jaw, each lock made to look as soft and silky as real life.

But it wasn't the magic of the Kind One's hands that held the girl enraptured. It was the magic of his voice. And when he came to the end of his telling, she sat a while in silence, soaking in his words, half wondering if he would continue.

At last, when no more story proved forthcoming, she said, "That was very sad."

"Yes," the Kind One agreed. "It was a sad time. A brutal time." He turned to her then, chisel in hand, and smiled his beautiful smile. She felt as though she basked in the light of her own personal sun. "But it's not the whole of the story. Come back tomorrow, and I will tell you more."

"Can you not tell me more now?" she asked. Later she would think back on this conversation and be surprised at her own daring. But at the time she felt so at ease in the Kind One's presence that she never thought to check her words.

The Kind One shook his head gently. "Your mother will already be wondering what has kept you so long. She'll worry about bear and wolves."

The girl doubted this very much. Her mother was far too busy to worry about her every child, certainly not in so short a time. Nevertheless she got to her feet, brushing wood shavings from her skirt. As she did so, she stepped outside the circle of light cast by the lantern . . . and suddenly became aware of the hugeness of the incomplete hall around her. High overhead, she heard the ringing of the Strong One's hammer. The sound touched her ears, bearing with it the return of all her fears.

She snatched up the empty waterskin and fled through the dark hall, making for the open western doors as fast as her short legs could carry her. She did not feel the Kind One's watching gaze follow her as she ran. Oblivious to all save her fear, she slipped through the doors and left the shadows of the hall behind, stepping into the late afternoon sunlight on the top of the promontory. Even then she felt no ease. Her fear pursued her, reaching from the hall to snatch her back.

So the girl continued her flight, darting through the rubble of construction and gaining the path down the hill and the sheltering arms of the forest. She kept her back to the Great House, focusing all her will on the trail before her, the trail leading back down to a life she knew and understood.

"I won't go back," she told herself. If her mother tried to send her, well, she'd dawdle and dispose of the water and return an appropriate amount of time later. She wouldn't lie. She simply wouldn't say anything, and she knew her mother, distracted by each day's cares, wouldn't ask. But the girl would never return and face the Brothers again, not on her own.

She paused suddenly as a glimmer caught her eye. Slowing her frantic pace, she moved to the side of the trail, peering through the tangle of leaves down to the river winding below. River Hanna, the life's blood of her people. From this vantage she could see fishermen in canoes returning to Kallias with the day's catch. She could see women crouched in water to their knees, scrubbing garments or filling skins.

But the girl's eyes trailed to the shore beyond and the unknown forest stretching as far as she could see. She whispered to herself, "The tribe across the river . . ."

And she wondered.

Mother did not ask her to return the next day. Nor the day after. Nor the day after that. The girl told herself that perhaps she wouldn't have to return, and even insisted she was glad.

But on the morning of the fourth day, as she followed her grandmother slowly down to the river—Grandmother often needed a younger shoulder for support—she found herself gazing across to the far bank again, even as she had on her way down from the Great House. While helping her grandmother to wash her face and arms and hands, she suddenly asked, "Were there people living across the river when you were a little girl?"

Grandmother raised her fair brows, wrinkles piling up on her forehead. She was the oldest woman in Kallias, mother of many children, grandmother to many more. But even in her age she did not forget a single name or face. She spoke the girl's name softly. "Yes," she answered. "Yes, there were people who lived across the river back then. Rannul tribe."

"You knew them?" the girl asked.

"I knew them." Grandmother offered no more but held out her hands for the girl to pat dry with a bit of woven fleece. The girl was gentle, for her mother always told her, " *Your grandmother is not strong. You need to take care of her.*"

It was odd though—for all her grandmother's frailty, there was always such a light in her pale eyes. Even now, as the girl glanced shyly up into her grandmother's face, she saw that telltale glimmer. It reminded the girl rather startlingly of the Strong One upon the promontory.

"Where did you hear of Rannul?" Grandmother asked as the girl helped her to her feet and back up the wide track to the village. "Has someone been telling you stories?"

The girl nodded. Then, as though sharing a great secret, she said, "The Kind One."

"The Kind One?" Grandmother smiled, and her eyes lifted to the promontory and the walls of the Great House rising up above. "You mean Akilun?"

The girl nodded. "He told me a story. Or part of a story."

"About the Rannul tribe?"

"Yes. And a man named Draven."

At the sound of that name, Grandmother paused and leaned more heavily on her granddaughter's shoulder. Concerned, the girl studied her grandmother's face, watching for some sign of illness or fatigue. Instead she saw only that same smile, though perhaps softer than it had been a moment before. The old woman drew several shallow breaths before finally saying, "That is a story worth hearing. Would you tell it to me?"

Thus encouraged, the girl launched into her own version of the tale she had heard several days before. She knew she didn't recall some of the details correctly, but her grandmother never interrupted her, only listened and nodded and grunted with interest.

Drawing to an end, the girl finished with "He said there was more, but . . ."

"But?"

The girl hung her head. "I haven't gone back to hear it."

"Why not?"

"Mother hasn't sent me."

But Grandmother was no fool. She put out a hand to a nearby fallen log and slowly lowered herself down upon it. She extended her bad foot before her, allowing it to rest. Then she turned a shrewd gaze upon her granddaughter. "You are afraid."

The girl did not answer.

"Are you afraid of Akilun?"

"No. But . . ." The girl found she could not put words to her fear. She didn't understand it. And Grandmother's clear eyes made her feel suddenly ashamed. She doubted her grandmother ever feared anything in her life. It wasn't in her nature.

Grandmother reached out and took the girl's hand. "Ask your mother," she said. "Ask her if you may carry the water gift today. And see what more Akilun has to tell you of Rannul tribe. Of Draven."

The girl stared at her grandmother's blue-veined hand, at the gnarled knuckles so weak with age. Grandmother squeezed, a certain urgency lending strength to her grip.

"Will you go, child?"

"I will go, Grandmother."

If Mother was surprised at the girl's request, she was in far too much of a hurry to show it. She was always in a hurry about something. Twelve children have a way of keeping a woman on her feet.

"Yes, yes!" she said, waving a hand at the full waterskin in her daughter's arms. "Yes, take it up, and be certain you don't bother the Brothers."

The girl wondered, as she climbed the track up the hill, if asking the Kind One to continue his story would be considered a bother. She pondered this same question all the way to the top of the promontory and stood a while on the edge of the wide clearing, staring up at the House, still pondering. She spied neither of the two Brothers from where she stood, but she could hear the sounds of their labors coming from inside.

On trembling feet she drew near to the great western doors once more. This time she could not spare a glance for their fantastical carvings. Her gaze was fixed entirely on the black shadows within. Shadows that seemed to creep out through the opening like dark, grasping hands.

"Hullo there."

The girl startled and whirled about. She found herself staring up at the Kind One, who stood before her with the sun in his hair. He smiled, and she felt her ramming heart grow calm, her breath come more easily.

"I wondered if you would return," Akilun said, putting out a hand to accept the water gift. He drank and then called to his brother. Etanun's muffled voice answered from within, declaring that he would be some time yet. Akilun shrugged and handed the skin back to the girl. "Can you wait?" he asked. "Until my brother has time to spare?"

The girl nodded. She wanted very much to ask about the continued story, but shyness clogged her throat. She hugged the waterskin to her chest and stared down at Akilun's feet. Did he even remember his promise to continue the tale?

But the Kind One did not leave her in suspense for long. He said,

"Would you like to see how my carving is progressing?"

Without looking up, the girl nodded. She slipped her hand into Akilun's and allowed him to lead her to the doors. Once more, while holding his hand, she found that the darkness of the great hall did not frighten her as it did when she stood alone. She passed through the doors into the massive space within, and it was like stepping into another world. A shadowy world, but full of secret beauty. If she only had different eyes, perhaps she would be able to see it and understand it. But even half-blind and uncomprehending, she thrilled at the possibilities and promises held within these mighty walls. She glimpsed the Strong One's powerful form partway up a supporting pillar but could not see what work he pursued.

The Kind One led her through piles of work rubble to that place along the northern wall where his lantern gleamed brightly on the contours of the ugly log. On the contours of Draven's face and neck and shoulders.

The girl gasped at the sight and let go of Akilun's hand in order to draw near. She stood just beside the lantern, felt the warmth of its glow on her skin. But her eyes were for the carving alone. For Draven. She could see every curl in his beard and thought that if she were only tall enough she could feel the softness of the fur mantle taking shape around his shoulders. Once more she had a sense of familiarity as she gazed upon his likeness, but she could not place it. There was not a man in all Kallias so strong, so noble, so sad.

She turned to the Kind One then, her curiosity making her bold. "What happened?" she asked, her voice bright and eager. "What happened to Draven? To the prisoner he would not kill?"

Akilun drew nearer to the girl and his work. He carried his hammer and chisel but did not set either to the log, not yet. He stood eye to eye with the wooden face he had carved.

"Let me tell you a story," he began.

SHADOW ON
THE WATER

E DID NOT KNOW where his footsteps took him, only that they carried him away, far away from the village center. Not to his own small house, nor even to the house of his mother where, when he was still a child, he had found comfort. His mother, were she still alive, would surely not receive him now. Her shame would be deeper even than his father's, for she would know that a coward had sprung from her womb.

So Gaho—Draven now, his shoulders bowed under the weight of his new name—stumbled through the shadows of swift-spreading dawn into the fields beyond the village cluster. In retrospect he hoped he had not trampled any of the crops so dearly precious to the life of Rannul, so hard won from the cold earth. But at the time he did not think of this. He merely walked, his vision dark even as he followed the sun's lengthening light.

He came at last to a fallow field far beyond the sight of any in the village. Not even the field workers, muddy-fingered women and children with curious, resentful eyes, would see him this far out. The grass of this field had grown high, shielding whole societies of small animals and insects in its depths. Into this world Draven plunged, the tall grass bowing beneath each step but springing back almost into proper shape behind him so that his progress was well shielded.

He collapsed in the center, prostrate and unmoving, and there lay for he knew not how long. It may have been hours later before the first real thought came into his head and whispered through his tightly drawn lips:

"What have I done?"

It was an honest question. Just then he couldn't remember. Even as he lay still and struggled to recall, he could form no clear vision of the events beyond his fight with the prisoner. He knew only that he had failed. He knew only that he bore the coward's name.

He knew that he had not finished the task set to him.

What could his future be? He saw many visions pass before his mind's eye. Visions of Gaher and the warriors of Rannul marching off to glorious battle . . . and Draven remaining behind. Remaining with the women and the children and the elderly warriors who spat upon his shadow whenever he passed them by. For no true men of Rannul would permit a coward to march in their midst.

His shame would stain him for the rest of his days. And what long, endless, tormented days awaited him!

He could not face them now. So he lay in the tall grass, so still that a line of ants marched over his hand and away. A grouse passed so near, he could have reached out and wrung its neck had he been able to summon the strength. A fox's long nose and bright eyes appeared in his vision, and it seemed to Draven that its gaze was full of disgust. It moved on silently into the tall grass, leaving Draven alone with the ants.

Perhaps he slept. That, or he fell into a sort of stupor. However it was, he grew so numb to the world that he did not hear or feel someone approach behind him and believed himself alone until a sudden sharp kick planted itself in his thigh.

With a jump that sent the poor industrious ants flying, Draven spun around, his fists clenched. He was prepared for the other young men of Rannul to hunt him down and try to make sport of him for his failure, and he knew in that instant that he would not succumb and permit them the pleasure, no matter how richly he deserved it. He would defend himself, coward though he was.

But it wasn't any of his fellows who stood above him now, face shadow-masked. It was his sister, leaning upon her branch. He should have heard her dragging footsteps reverberate through the ground on which his ear was pressed. And yet here he crouched, his thigh aching where she'd kicked it, staring up at her in surprise.

"Gaho," she began, "you must help."

"No," said Draven, his voice a growl. He sank down, relaxing once more into his despair, knees up, elbows propped, fists uncurling. He shook his head, and his hair fell into his eyes. "Not Gaho. I am Draven now. You heard our father make it so."

Ita studied him silently, shifting her stance to take pressure from her ugly clubfoot. Despite the calluses and the wrappings of animal hide, it hurt her each time she took a step. In a rare moment of vulnerability Ita had told Draven that to put any weight upon that foot was to send scalding embers crawling up the inside of her bone. But after that whispered confession he had never heard her complain again. The villagers proclaimed it a marvel that she had ever learned to walk at all.

Many had urged her father to dispose of her life quickly and kindly when she was still a swaddled babe, thus preventing both her lifelong suffering and the burden she was bound to be upon her people.

But Gaher had listened to her powerful cries and watched how she latched onto her mother and fed like a ravening wolf cub. And he had declared that she was a wolf indeed and would make him proud one day, twisted foot or otherwise. So, in a mingling of mercy and pride, he had spared her life.

Ita had yet to earn her woman's name. But it was possible already to see a woman's strength in the gaze she turned upon her brother just then. She offered him neither sympathy nor scorn, but her eyes urged him to action. He found that he resented her. Were it not for her words before his trial began, he would even now be a true man.

Moving with care, Ita balanced herself on her good leg and reached out with her branch to prod Draven's calf. He wanted to snatch that branch away from her and break it in two. But she was his sister, and he kept his fury in check.

"Draven, then," she said. "You must help. I've heard such . . . such terrible things."

Draven did not respond. He didn't care what she had heard. He could guess at what was being said among the people of Rannul.

But Ita persisted, her voice growing ever more tense as she spoke. "They're going to punish him. To punish him for your mercy. At sunfall they're going to—" Her voice broke, but the tremor told Draven all he needed to know. The old warriors had spoken before in his hearing of the interesting torments worked upon especially despised prisoners of war. He had yet to see it done, but he knew what pain every man—every *true* man—of Rannul was capable of inflicting. Pain that would continue long after the sufferer begged for death.

"They're going to punish him for living," Ita said, "when they believe he should be dead."

They would spill their rage upon the head of a Kahorn man rather than on the more deserving head of their chieftain's son. But it would not assuage Draven's guilt.

"I should have killed him," Draven said, still unable to raise his gaze, to look his sister in the eye. "It is my fault. He has lived beyond his time, and now he will pay the blood price in agony. I should have killed him."

"But you didn't," Ita said. "And his life is now yours by right. Will you let it be so harshly treated? So abused and then wasted?"

Draven shrugged. "I gave up all right to his life when I refused to end it."

Silence hung upon the air between them, filled only with the buzz of insects and the gentle *shush* of wind in the grass. Even the village was strangely quiet on this day of stunned humiliation.

Then Ita kicked him. She always kicked him with her clubfoot, for she needed the good one for balance. Draven knew that each kick, delivered with far more habitual accuracy than he liked, must hurt her a great deal, but this never seemed to stop her. She kicked him in the shin, startling him from his dour thoughts, pushing him into a flash of irritation. "Ow!" he growled, his eyes darting to her face.

Ita growled right back, her lips curled back. "If you won't be a man, at least be my brother!" she said. "I know you, Gaho. Draven. Whoever you are, I know you, and I know you will not sit here in this forsaken field and let time crawl over you while the rest of us live and die. I *know* you, brother, and you are going to help me. You are going to help me deliver the prisoner back to his own people and prevent the—the things the men are saying. His life is yours whether or not you acknowledge it. And you *will* acknowledge it, and you *will* protect it!"

Draven wrapped his arms around his legs, guarding against future assaults. "Why do you care?" he demanded. "Why do you care what happens to one man from across the river? He's not of our blood! He means nothing."

"Perhaps," Ita said slowly, her voice less furious than it had been but no less passionate. "But I do care. I care for your sake. The wounds they inflict upon him tonight will scar *you* forever. I do not wish to see that happen."

She crouched before him then and, setting aside her branch, put out her hands and caught his face. He did not resist as she turned his gaze to meet hers. They were very alike, this brother and sister, easily recognized as kin. But while his face was strong and filled out, hers was always a little wan, a little peaked, with hollows under her eyes that betrayed unspoken suffering. But the eyes themselves glittered with a potency not even her bear-like brother could match.

"Help me," she said. "I cannot do this on my own. But if you will not help me, I will try."

"You will fail," Draven whispered.

"But I will try."

She held onto him a moment longer, forcing him to read the truth in her eyes. At last he drew a deep breath and gently removed her hands from his face, though he held onto them and rose, assisting her to her feet. He stood more than a head taller than she, for though he had only just that day become a man, he had already grown into his man's height, if not yet his full breadth. And she would never be any taller or stronger than a child.

"Where are they keeping the prisoner?" Draven asked.

"In your house," Ita replied.

He had built the house with his own two hands, and he knew all of its secrets. He knew the two soft places in the wall where the sod was loose and could easily be knocked through. It was customary among his people to build houses in this way, with only one entrance but several possible exists known only to the builder himself. One never knew when such exits would be necessary.

The sun was already high in the sky, and there was little cover to be had. But Draven's house was built on the edge of Rannul village, for he had craved privacy at that time, his solitary nature eager for quiet after years of living in the large boys' house near the village center. The men of the village, save for the guard set round the temporary prison, were all gathered at the central fire, chanting, praying, and vowing to each other what they would accomplish when the sun went down and could not bear witness to their dark deeds.

But there was a guard of four, one posted at each corner of the house. So Draven, crouched out of sight in a nearby thicket of fir trees, waited for Ita to accomplish her nefarious purpose.

She hobbled boldly through the village, nodding solemnly to her father and making signs of reverence as she passed by the men around the fire. Her progress was slow, for the weight of the waterskin she carried impeded her use of her walking stick. But no one moved to assist her. No one dared, for Ita was possessed of a sharp tongue and never shy to use it when she suspected anyone of belittling her.

So she proceeded in plain sight toward Draven's house. All four guards saw her coming and turned to face her. Even then Draven dared not make a move but waited to see what she would do.

"I am come to visit my father's enemy," Ita declared and lifted the heavy waterskin for the guards to see. "I will give him refreshment."

"No," said the foremost guard.

"His wounds are untreated, and he will surely die," Ita persisted. "Let me through."

The guard said nothing. His three fellows took a few paces from their appointed posts. Ita looked at them all, her gaze sliding from one face to the next. Then she adjusted her grip on the waterskin and started for the door.

The foremost guard intercepted her, putting out a staying hand. Ita flashed her teeth at him. "Do you want him dead before sunfall? Let me pass!"

The guards exchanged glances. One looked out to Gaher in the village center, who sat cross-legged in deep, dark meditation, his crescent ax, still stained with blood, across his knees. It would take more uproar by far to disturb the warriors of Rannul in their preparations for the coming night. The guards could expect no support from that quarter.

"You may not see the prisoner," the foremost guard insisted.

"I *will*," Ita replied. No woman of Rannul would dare speak to a man in such a voice, certainly no girl who had yet to earn her woman's name. But Ita was not like others her age. And she was more than a little intimidating, despite her size and crippled foot. She took another step, prepared to force her way through. The foremost guard caught at her shoulder, and she shrugged off his tentative hand. The other three drew in closer now, forming a wall between her and her goal . . .

. . . while Draven slipped from the fir trees and, moving quietly despite his bulk, crossed the distance to his own house and pulled away the loose sod of the back wall.

Though he had slept here only the night before, the four walls of his chamber had become foreign to him in such a short space of time. Draven crawled through the opening he created, shivering at the stench of man's blood. There was little light save that which came through the smoke-hole in the roof, but this was enough to illuminate the form of the prisoner lying bound upon Draven's own bed, the blood from his shoulder matting in the sheepskin rugs. The prisoner lay so still that Draven wondered if he was dead already. A mercy if he was!

But no sooner had this thought crossed Draven's mind than the prisoner's eyes opened, bright in the dimness of that room. He said nothing, but his gaze fixed upon Draven without recognition. A shudder passed through his body, and he struggled to push himself upright, though his strength was far gone and his skin ghastly pale.

Draven crossed the room and knelt before him, a finger to his lips. An instant later the prisoner's expression shifted to one of recognition. And fear. Had his burly enemy come to finish the task he had failed to accomplish a few hours ago?

"I'll not harm you," Draven whispered, answering the unspoken question. "Not unless you force my hand."

"Liar," the prisoner said, adding a painful curse. "Why else would you come?"

Why else indeed? Draven sighed. Then he motioned to the small opening in the back of the house. "Your freedom is nigh. Come with me."

"Freedom to die by your hand?"

"Would you prefer that which you know awaits you come sunfall?"

The prisoner's jaw set, but the shadows on his face could not disguise the sickening in his soul. Nevertheless he said, "I'm not afraid to meet my fate."

"Now who lies?" said Draven. "But it is not the act of a coward to flee his captors if given the chance. Come. Someone told me that your life belongs to me. If that is so, I choose that you should live it. You'll not have a second offer."

The prisoner hesitated briefly. Then he heaved himself up from the low bed and turned to allow Draven to cut his bonds away. Draven felt the tension in the prisoner's body, every muscle braced for a killing stroke. Though the temptation flitted through Draven's mind, he knew still what he had learned about himself at dawn that day: He was no killer.

So he cut the prisoner free and, listening to Ita's ongoing argument with the guards without (which began to wax most dramatic and verbose), Draven pushed his new charge ahead of him out the escape hole and into the open world beyond. Their danger was perhaps at its greatest in that brief space as they crossed from the house into the fir trees and the wild lands beyond. If Ita failed to hold the attention of the guards and an alarm went up, Draven suspected he would share the prisoner's fate. His father would not move to intercede.

But they achieved the shelter of the firs and plunged on into the deeper forest beyond the fields and roughly cultivated lands of Rannul village. Draven knew where he must take the prisoner and there hide him until nightrise. A small culvert in a secret hollow where solitary young Gaho had often fled for much-craved quiet during his boyhood days. No one knew of this spot save perhaps Ita. (He never could guess just how much his sister knew.) Draven had a canoe moored there which would slide easily into the river, far downstream from where the hunt for the prisoner would begin. First the men of Rannul would check their own canoes and make certain none were missing. Then they would spread out into the forests and fields, little thinking that their quarry might have other means to cross the river back into Kahorn territory.

None would suspect Chief Gaher's son of the treachery he even now committed.

The prisoner stumbled. Then he stumbled again, and his pace slackened more than Draven liked. Draven could not know when the search would begin, could only hope the prisoner's loss would not be discovered until the sun was well on its way to rest. They may have hours, but they may have mere seconds.

The prisoner sank to his knees. His blood loss was too great for such exertion. Another moment and he would surely faint outright.

Grinding his teeth to suppress a doglike growl, Draven caught up the prisoner and slung him across his shoulders. The man was heavy but not too heavy, and Draven moved swiftly through the trees, off the beaten paths and into the deeper forest. He followed River Hanna downstream, keeping it ever on his right hand. The prisoner's blood soaked into his own garments; he would have to rinse them as best he could before returning to Rannul. At least none in the village would look to find the chieftain's disgraced son again for several days. Draven's absence would be less noticed than expected.

His path took him uphill, and yet Draven bore his burden for some while before he began to lose breath. His was a strength to make a father proud, which only added to his shame. The prisoner was so limp and lifeless in his hold that Draven wondered if he had died. Good, if so! Someone should have died that dawn. Blood should have been spilt to appease the airy gods.

A low agonized moan told Draven that these wishes were vain. The prisoner may only just cling to life, but cling he did.

The river was now far below Draven's feet, cutting through rocky outcroppings and careening at a wild, white pace through a harsher landscape than what lay further upstream. No one among the Rannul tribe took their watercraft this far downriver at this time of year. Only during the season when Hydrus was said to return and all the proud warriors sought to slay him did they dare risk the rapids in this quest. This time of year, months before any sighting of Hydrus might be hoped for, Draven did not fear meeting his tribal kin.

He came to a place where the ground gave way, dropping in deep rocky walls down to the culvert below. Many little streams rolled downhill to this place, plunging here and there in thin white spray to crash on the rocks, break into the culvert, and rush away into the rapids.

An unfamiliar eye would not spy a path down, but Draven knew this spot quite well. He had never made this descent while so heavily burdened, however.

Draven slid the prisoner from his shoulders into the dry rustle of the forest floor. The prisoner's eyes were open but glassy, and he collapsed under his own weight and did not move save to breathe.

"On your feet," Draven said. "You're not safe yet."

At first he thought the prisoner would not respond. But then, with a shudder of resisting muscles, the young man pushed himself upright. Leaning heavily on Draven's supporting arm—their enmity for the moment forgotten in the face of necessity—he allowed himself to be led to the cliff's edge and down along the narrow track. If he wished to protest he swallowed it back, though his eyes became briefly more alert as they gazed upon the drop and the far-falling streams.

Draven led him carefully, however his conscience demanded otherwise. Sometimes he half-carried him and once caught him by the arm when the prisoner's foot slipped on a moss-clad rock. But at last they reached the banks below and took shelter with their backs to the cliff wall, their feet close to the flowing water. Draven could see that the prisoner, along with his other many ills, was cold. Gooseflesh rose along his arms, and his bare feet were strangely blue.

Grunting, Draven removed his fur mantle and wrapped it around the prisoner. Bile rose in the back of his throat even as he performed this action. No true man was he to treat his enemy thus!

And so they waited.

Ita's voice fell gently from above, drawing Draven from his intense contemplation of the moving water at his feet. He turned where he sat and looked up, surprised. There was his sister's pale face gazing down at him from above. So she did know his secret after all.

"Wait, Ita!" he cried and scrambled to his feet, hastening up the narrow path before she tried to discover it for herself. She was never one to ask for help, and he did not doubt that she'd fall and break her neck before admitting she could not see the way.

By the unpredictable grace of the airy gods, Ita did as she was bidden and waited for Draven to reach her. "What are you doing here?" Draven demanded as soon as he was close enough to be heard without shouting.

She shrugged one shoulder, over which was slung a sack. "The prisoner was wounded," she said. "He'll not survive a day's walk back to his village unless the wound is bound."

Draven could not argue. Judging from the rigid lines of pain he had witnessed settling across the prisoner's face, he doubted even Ita's ministrations would bolster him enough for such a trek. But the fellow would not die in Rannul territory at least.

Ita followed her brother down the narrow track, her branch tapping the rocks ahead of her to test their dependability. Draven did not touch her, though he longed to take her arm and support her along the way. Ita would not stand for that. So he moved slowly, allowing her plenty of time to pick her way behind him. In this manner they reached the prisoner at last.

The prisoner gazed dully up at Ita. There were faint questions in his eyes, but he was too weak to ask any of them. When Ita opened her sack and set to cleaning and binding his wound, he closed his eyes and leaned back his head, the muscles in his neck straining now and then. But he made no protest.

When she'd finished, Ita rose to her feet, grimacing as she was forced to put weight upon her clubfoot. She leaned against the wall and turned to Draven, her eyes flashing as though daring him to comment on her pain. "Are you waiting for nightrise?" she asked.

"Yes."

She glanced out at the white rapids. "You'll not navigate that in the dark."

"Safer than setting out now and being seen."

"Have you done it before?"

"Yes."

"At night?"

Draven did not reply. Taking this as answer enough, Ita sighed and shook her head, her pale hair falling across her face. Then she said, "I'll go with you. I'll sit in the prow with a light."

"No," said Draven. "That would only confuse my vision. The moon will rise, and I'll use her light alone."

Ita looked as though she wished to argue. Thinking better of it, she said only, "I'll go with you."

And Draven, who knew his sister well, kept his mouth shut.

Darkness came soon enough, filling the hollow and spreading across the forest. The prisoner's loss would now be known across Rannul, and the search would spread over the fields and into the wilds. Still Draven waited, his sister beside him, the prisoner at their feet. It was too dark to see their faces, and Draven was glad.

Far away they heard the beat of Rannul drums. A beat of summoning. A beat of rage.

The moon rose. By her light, the culvert became eerily bright. Draven moved to a secret place along the bank and pulled back a sheep's hide covered over with bits of moss and rocks and leaves. Beneath it lay his canoe, built of his own hands. It was smaller than the war canoes of Gaher's men, but it was well balanced. There was space enough in the bottom for the prisoner to lie, and Draven helped him to climb inside. Once there, however, the prisoner insisted on sitting upright.

"Can you shift your weight at need?" Draven demanded.

"My people know the waterways," the prisoner replied. His voice boasted more strength than previously; perhaps Ita's healing hand had worked better magic than Draven had believed. "I will not overturn us."

Draven grunted and began to slide the canoe into the water. Ita, moving with surprising grace, sprang forward, ready to climb aboard as well. But Draven was too quick for her. He stepped between her and his craft, pushed off into the culvert, and leapt inside.

"Gaho!" Ita cried, forgetting her brother's new name in her fury. "Come back for me!"

"Forgive me, Ita," Draven called over his shoulder, and left her standing on the bank even as he took up his paddle. There was no time for more words, no time for arguments. The water flowing from the culvert spilled into the rapids, dragging the canoe with it. The prisoner clutched the sides of the canoe, shifting his weight with expert coordination, Draven was grateful to note. Otherwise, they may well have ended their journey rather more abruptly than planned.

Navigating from memory as much as by the eerie moonlight, Draven struck out with his paddle and avoided the rocks. He knew that the rapids, while treacherous, would likely not be able to take his life even if he were overturned. He was a strong swimmer and had survived a broken canoe or two while learning these waters. But the prisoner would not be so lucky, not in his wounded condition. No, there was no quarter for mistakes, not tonight.

Draven felt the familiar thrill in his gut as the first of the longer plunges took them. Cold spray soaked their skin, soaked through the dressings on the prisoner's shoulder. Draven watched him, crouched in the prow of the canoe, his pain forgotten in the need for precise balance.

The second plunge was greater than the first, and for a terrifying instant Draven feared that he had lost control. His memory failed him, and he felt unfamiliar panic. But his arms recalled what his head could not, and on instinct he struck out and narrowly avoided crushing boulders. He heard the scrape of his canoe, felt the pressure of solid rock beneath his feet. But the river pulled his craft over and away, and no damage was worked . . . no lethal damage anyway.

Once, and only once, the prisoner cried out. He did not know these treacherous waters and could scarcely see the way before him. A single cry was not the sign of a coward, and Draven felt his respect for his enemy rising. He himself made no sound, all his efforts concentrating on their survival.

Thank the airy gods he had left Ita behind! She would flay him with her tongue should he live to return. But that would be better by far than seeing her dashed to pieces in this crushing flow.

The third plunge was not so deep, but it was fast and winding. Draven half-stood in the canoe, his bare feet braced on the sides. How deceptively calm the water looked in the moonlight, belying the dangerous currents beneath! But Draven did not lose his head. He shouted to the prisoner, "Lean!" though he had no time to call a direction. He could only trust that the prisoner, feeling the pull of Hanna's frothy arms, would be able to interpret the command correctly.

The prisoner leaned—to the right, just as needed. The canoe tipped frightfully, but Draven's push on the left-hand boulder created just the right balance and slid them through the narrow pass unharmed. The instant they were through, both Draven and the prisoner ducked low, arms outspread, striving to attain the necessary equilibrium again and not overturn the canoe.

Thus they burst free of the rapids. Draven the coward sat upright as the calmer, deeper waters of wide Hanna welcomed them and cradled them in her chilly bosom. He turned to look back over his shoulders, watching the moonlight touch the white foam of the rapids and turn it to living silver. As far as he knew, no other man had done what he and his enemy had just accomplished. Too bad that he was no true man and the prisoner no better than a devil.

The prisoner himself collapsed in the bottom of the canoe and did not move, his remaining strength momentarily lost to him. But he had proven a worthy water-mate, Draven admitted. And he wondered briefly what the two of them might have achieved together had they been born of the same village. Perhaps they may have even hunted Hydrus in his season.

Draven continued to paddle, his heart slowing to match the steady rhythm of his arms. The prisoner did not move, but his heavy breathing told Draven that he did live. Kahorn territory encompassed the whole of the opposite bank, as far as Draven knew. He searched for a safe mooring.

Suddenly the prisoner sat up. The canoe tilted, and Draven was obliged to shift his paddle and weight to regain balance once more. The prisoner, who had been so careful while they navigated the rapids, did not seem to notice. The light of the pale moon illuminated his upturned face.

He stared up at a high, bare promontory on the Kahorn side of Hanna. Draven had seen this promontory before but never thought much of it beyond the strange fact that nothing grew upon its slopes, though the surrounding landscape was lush with forests. He had never experienced anything like the dread that he now saw etching lines in the prisoner's face. Curious, Draven looked up to those high crags himself.

He saw, much to his surprise, that the promontory was not so bare as he had supposed. By the light of the moon he saw the thin arms of a dead tree right on the very summit.

"The shadow!"

Draven startled at the prisoner's voice. He looked at his pale face again, and found that the prisoner had turned imploring eyes upon him. Not once during their death-brawl the night before had Draven glimpsed such a desperate expression on the other man's face, not even when he anticipated the final blow. It was strange and unnerving.

"The shadow," the prisoner said. "Don't let us pass through the shadow." He pointed to the long reach of the promontory's dark silhouette cast across the water.

Draven did not think to argue. There was too much awful urgency in the prisoner's voice. So he changed their course and drew the canoe up closer to Rannul territory, where the shadow did not reach. They slipped past, and Draven moved to the center of the river again.

"Please," said the prisoner, "carry me on."

"Will that not take you far from your village?" Draven asked. The prisoner must have been caught many miles upstream, and the further they went now, the longer his trek home would be.

"It does not matter," said the prisoner. "Please." Once more he looked back over his shoulder at the promontory, now behind them.

Again, Draven did not argue but continued paddling in silence. The world around them spoke in the voices of the night, and the river's songs whispered to them until the promontory was almost lost in the darkness. At length the prisoner said, "Here," and pointed to a sandy bank on the Kahorn side of Hanna.

Draven steered his craft to it, plunging the prow of the canoe up onto the sand. The prisoner climbed out, staggering in his weakness. Draven remained where he was. He half expected the prisoner to run, disappearing without another word into the forests, never to be seen again.

Instead, the prisoner stood with his back to Draven for several breaths. His wounded arm, exhausted from the strain it had endured over the rapids, shuddered with pain.

"My name is Callix," he said suddenly, turning and looking Draven in the eye. "Prince of Kahorn."

"I know," said Draven.

"Because I am alive, your father will wage war upon my people." Callix kept his eyes fixed upon Draven's. "You must dissuade him."

"Gaher will never be dissuaded." Certainly not by his coward son.

"You must try. For your people's sake."

Here Draven drew himself up, his eyes alight. Disgraced though he was, the pride of Rannul still ran in his veins. "My people are not afraid of war. Certainly not against Kahorn!"

But Callix shook his head solemnly. "You don't understand. You *must not* let them cross the river. If they do, they will suffer the same fate as Kahorn. And that is not a fate you would wish upon even us, your age-old enemies."

Draven felt some of the pride-rage dying back in place of curiosity. "What can you mean by this?" he demanded. "From what do your people suffer? Why were you found so far from your village?" He paused, then added, "And why do you fear that high hill?"

Callix stepped back, his eyes very dark as the shadows of the forest closed in around him, blocking out the moonlight. "Ask me no questions, Gaher's son. You have saved my life . . . let me return the favor with my warning. Do not cross the river. Not in war. Not in peace."

With those words, the Prince of Kahorn slipped away and was gone, leaving Draven with the prow of his canoe upon the sandy bank.

A SLOW CLIMB

A S THE KIND ONE SPOKE—working on his woodcarving all the while—it seemed to the girl that his voice came from far away. Indeed, as his story progressed she began to feel as though she herself stepped from the confines of her body and drifted on the winds of time to years gone by. Akilun's words bore her up and carried her gently back to an age before Kallias Village was built, back to a time when a warlike tribe lived across the river. She thought she saw Rannul Village from her high vantage, and the field where Draven lay prostrate in despair. She thought she saw brave, clubfooted Ita tending to the wounds of her enemy, and the white rush of River Hanna's rapids.

The girl did not know it, but the images she beheld so clearly in her mind's eye were the result of Akilun's speech. For as he spun his tale, he did not speak in the language of the girl's tribe but in his own tongue. And that was a language the girl did not understand but which struck her ear and broke in her mind, scattering into images, sounds, smells, tastes, all manner of sensations which she could understand deep down in her heart and soul. Had she been even a year or two older, she may have noticed the strangeness of the Kind One's telling and been too afraid to go on listening. As it was, she sat in rapt attention as the story played out before her vision.

But when Akilun spoke of the promontory and the dead tree standing upon its crown, something stranger still happened to the girl's vision. She was staring, without realizing that she did so, at the stump Akilun carved. Not at the carving of Draven's immobile, ageless face, but at the stump itself. When Akilun told how Draven looked up and saw the tree's warped branches etched in moonlight, it seemed to the girl that she was Draven herself, seeing with his eyes. The ugly stump before her was no stump at all but sprouted great branches such as it must have boasted in the days before it was hewn down. These twisted in the shadows, reaching beyond the light of the Kind One's lantern. Reaching like hands to touch the girl's face.

She gasped and sat up straight, her eyes staring. The stump was only a stump once more, and Draven's too-familiar eyes gazed down upon her. But in her imagination the girl could still see, like ghosts, where the branches had been.

Akilun paused in his work, setting aside his hammer and chisel. "I think perhaps that is enough story for one day," he said, smiling gently at the girl. His smile comforted her, and the ghostly branches vanished from her view.

Nevertheless, she was grateful when Akilun took her hand and led her back through the cavernous hall—beneath the ringing work of the Strong One's hammer overhead—to the great double doors. The sunlight welcomed her, and she stepped, blinking, into the work-littered yard.

"Will you come again tomorrow?" Akilun asked as he let go of her hand.

The girl looked up at him. Beyond his shining face she saw the darkness of the hall. Her heart beat a conflicted rhythm in her breast. She both shook and nodded her head and could not have told which answer was true.

Then she ducked her chin to her chest and darted away, seeking the path back down to Kallias.

"Did you see Akilun?" her grandmother asked when the girl settled down next to the old woman at the family fire that night. "Did he tell you more of the story?"

The girl nodded, staring into the dancing flames without seeing them. She watched instead the black wood held in the heart of the fire, its dry bark wrinkling back to reveal the heartwood beneath. She wondered if trees felt pain.

"What did he tell you?" her grandmother urged. Her voice was low, and she spoke for the girl's ears alone. The rest of the family group was caught up in the tale of the day's hunt as spun by the girl's eldest sister. No one had spare attention to give the quiet little girl and her old grandmother.

The girl was glad for her grandmother's interest. It was hard to earn much notice when part of so large a family. But she found herself hesitant to speak of what she'd heard that day.

Her very hesitancy was enough for her discerning grandmother, however. The old woman nodded and said a quiet, "Ah!" before leaning closer to the girl and putting an arm around her shoulders. "I know. I know," she said softly. "It is a difficult tale, that one. Did he speak of the tree?"

Surprised, the girl turned a sharp glance up to her grandmother's face.

"Yes," the old woman said, reading all the answer she needed in that one quick look. "I thought as much. Be brave, dear child, and hear the tale to its end. Has Akilun spoken of Hydrus yet, and of the great hunt?"

"No, grandmother."

"Well then, tomorrow I shall go up the hill with you and ask Akilun to tell the tale. I have not heard that part of the story in a long while and would be glad to have it told me again."

So the girl leaned into her grandmother's side, glad that the decision was taken from her hands this time. She would have to climb the promontory tomorrow. She would have to help Grandmother.

"You are mad," the girl's mother said the next day, scowling as she held the full waterskin in her hands. "Quite mad. What do you think you're about, climbing the hill at your age?"

"At my age?" Grandmother laughed, her eyes sparkling merrily. "You'd put me in my grave, Iulia, but I'm not so ancient as all that."

"Ancient or otherwise, you'll do yourself an injury if you insist on such foolishness," her daughter replied, handing the waterskin to the girl as she spoke. "Think of your condition!"

"I do, more frequently than I like," Grandmother said mildly. "Which is why I'm bringing a strong young shoulder to lean on." So saying, she placed a hand on the girl's shoulder and gripped hard as though to prevent the girl from running off.

The girl's mother looked from her daughter to the old woman and back again. The girl could see her forming another argument and knew

---

that in another moment she would suggest Grandmother bring one of the stout young boys along with her instead. But in the end, Iulia simply threw up her hands and declared she hadn't the time to contend with such nonsense, and if the two of them wanted to waste a whole day on such an imprudent trek, so be it! She had mouths to feed and crops to gather and so on and so on.

So Iulia stalked off, still grumbling, and the girl and her grandmother exchanged secret smiles.

Partway up the hill, however, the girl began to wonder if her mother had been right. Grandmother was not as strong as she used to be, and her condition made the going very slow. To a certain extent, the girl didn't mind. She wasn't eager to face that ugly stump again, or Draven's wooden visage either, for that matter.

But the longer they took, the more opportunity fear had to take hold in her heart. By the time she and her grandmother finally reached the apex of the promontory and gazed upon the proud splendor of the Great House, the girl's steps were equally as slow and stumbling as the old woman's.

"Spirits of our fathers!" the old woman exclaimed as she gazed out from the trees' long shadows at the high walls and sweeping buttresses, the stone-carved eaves and cornices and the enormous double doors. The girl heard all the weariness lift from the old woman's voice, and indeed even her hand lightened its hold on the girl's shoulder as she straightened to stand nearly as tall as she had when she was young. "It is so very grand! I have not made this climb in many years, and it was beautiful then. But this! Ah!"—and here a dart of sorrow pierced her voice—"if only my poor husband had lived to see it so near completion."

The girl turned wide eyes up to her grandmother's face. She could not remember ever before hearing her grandmother speak of her husband. He had died many years ago, gathered to winter's cold embrace long before the girl was born. Iulia spoke of him fondly upon occasion when seated with the family around the evening fire. She called him a proud, brave man, a worthy chief of Kallias. But grandmother never mentioned his name.

Her old eyes were bright with unshed tears, however, as she gazed at the Great House before them. Then she shook her head, and pressure on the girl's shoulder urged her on into the yard.

Shading her eyes, the girl could see the Strong One about his work high on the topmost roof. He spotted them as well and acknowledged them with a wave of his arm. But he did not come down to receive his water-gift, being caught up in whatever task he currently pursued.

They found the Kind One on the south side of the Great House, the side nearest the promontory's precipitous cliff face. The girl saw the river far below, and her eyes scanned the swift-flowing water for signs of fishermen in their canoes, but spotted none. She thought of Draven and the prisoner and their mad flight in darkness, and wondered if any man of Kallias could boast as much courage as the coward and his enemy.

Akilun was dismantling a tall, fearfully unstable scaffold, but he stopped the moment he spied his visitors and climbed down to greet them.

"Good mother," he said, making the appropriate sign of respect as he approached, raising two fingers and tracing a half-circle in the air. One could almost believe he was himself a man of Kallias, so natural were his gestures and words. But no man of Kallias ever shone with such a strange, inexorable beauty that not even an overcast sky heavy with coming rain could suppress. "It is many years since we have seen one another."

"Mere moments to you," Grandmother replied, reaching out to place her own hand on his forehead, the familiar blessing the elderly of Kallias bestowed upon young warriors. "You have not aged a day, Akilun."

"Neither have you in your heart," Akilun said, his face resplendent with one of his lovely smiles. He turned that smile down upon the girl, who, suddenly shy, tucked herself closer to her grandmother. "Thank you for the water gift," he said.

Remembering her role, the girl held out the skin and watched as Akilun drank. When he was through, he peered up at the rooftop but could not spot his brother. "Etanun will be some while," he said, then addressed himself again to the girl and her grandmother. "Will you hear more of the story?"

"I understand," Grandmother said, "that you have yet to tell of the hunting of Hydrus."

"Indeed!" Akilun replied even as he handed the waterskin back to the girl's waiting arms. "Though I would be shy to do so in your company, good mother, for you may spin that tale far better than I!"

"Indeed not," said she with a shake of her head. "I have not heard it in many a year, and I fear I would forget the details."

Even as she spoke, thunder growled overhead and the heavy clouds, strained to the bursting point, began to spill over with drizzle.

"Please," said Akilun, offering a supporting hand. Grandmother lifted her weight from the girl's shoulder and leaned upon him instead as he escorted her into the shelter of the vast, echoing hall. The girl felt a little resentful as she followed along behind. After all, she had supported her grandmother all the way up the long climb.

At the doorway she paused. Without the comfort of Akilun's hand, she found she did not like to enter the shadows of the Great House, which seemed so much darker on this overcast day. But Akilun, sensing her hesitancy, paused and looked around. "I think your grandmother needs you," he said.

It wasn't true. Her grandmother was perfectly content leaning upon his arm. But the girl was grateful nonetheless, and slipped over to the old woman's side. So the three of them made their way across the hall toward the pool of light where the Kind One's lantern shone.

Grandmother gasped. "Oh great spirits! Oh great airy gods!"

The girl saw that her grandmother's eyes were fixed upon the carving of Draven. Akilun had made little progress on it since yesterday. It didn't matter. The eyes of that wooden face seemed to gaze out from beyond the confines of carving with an expression more alive, more intense than the girl remembered. Far more living than she comprehended or could ever articulate. She felt a tremor run through her grandmother's arm, and she knew that the old woman better understood what she saw, though even she could not understand completely.

She said only, "It is very like, I think."

"Yes," said Akilun, simply. He could accept the compliment on his skill, perhaps because he did not deem it either more or less than what it was. Overhead, the drum of rain echoed in the rafters, and a surreptitious *drip, drip, drip* revealed those places where the roof remained incomplete. But here, in the circle of lantern light, the dreariness of the day could not penetrate.

Akilun found something for the old woman to sit upon, and the girl stood at her side, still holding her hand. "Now tell me," Akilun said, taking up his hammer and chisel to continue his work, "where does the tale of this hunt begin?"

"You must say, Akilun," said the girl's grandmother. "I cannot remember."

"I believe that you do," the Kind One replied. "How could you forget?"

"The years work a curse of forgetfulness on those of my kind," Grandmother replied. "You have not the knowing of such loss, for all your experience and wisdom."

"But some things are never truly lost," Akilun said.

The girl found herself growing very impatient. "Please!" she said, though it was rude, she knew, to interrupt her elders. "Who was Hydrus? You have mentioned him many times now. Was he a man? An enemy of the tribes? Or a monster?"

"Oh no!" her grandmother replied, patting the girl's hand gently. "No, Hydrus was no enemy. Neither was he a monster. Hydrus was a gift." Her eyes rested upon the carving of Draven, and had the girl been asked, she would have said without hesitation that he gazed back at her.

"Let me tell you a story," her grandmother said.

THE HUNTING
OF HYDRUS

VERY MAN, WOMAN, and child of Rannul dreamed of
Hydrus. Little boys, as soon as they were old enough to sit
quietly and listen to a tale, would hear their grandfathers tell
long, complex, and fanciful accounts of hunts in years gone by. Little
girls, as soon as they were old enough to carve spears out of stout
saplings, would practice their aim, turning any ordinary object into a
target, dreaming they aimed for Hydrus's eye.

Hydrus himself lived in the ocean, far away beyond imagining.
Rannul boasted only faint memories passed down over many generations
of explorers who claimed to have seen the Endless Water beyond the
western horizon. It was there, the tale tellers said, that Hyrus lived, a
long, sinuous ribbon of darkness, small compared to the vast creatures

who swam those salty waters with him.

But when he made his cyclical journey up the River Hanna, penetrating deep into the heart of the great forest country—Ah! Then did Hydrus become a mighty king, monarch of the river.

He migrated with others of his kind far up the river to the freezing lake country beyond Rannul territory. Many hundreds of miles he traveled, but no perils there could threaten Hydrus. Not the great-clawed beasts that hunted from the shores, picking off his kindred and feasting on fleshy bounty—not the sharp-taloned raptors that swooped from the skies to snatch up his younger brothers and sisters and bear them away to towering nests—nay, not even the two-legged predators with their swift-darting lances and spears or their cunningly crafted nets—none of these could deter Hydrus from his instinctual course.

He traversed the waters of Hanna, as dark and winding as the very spirit of the river himself. And he feared neither man nor beast.

Indeed, Hydrus knew nothing of fear. In the last hundred years of his life he'd never had cause. Not even when a sharp-eyed young warrior—Gaher by name—had thrown a surer spear than those of his fellows and struck the old fish a mere finger's breadth from his eye. A flash of pain, perhaps, a brief but soon-forgotten wariness, and nothing more disturbed the murky stability of Hydrus's consciousness. He was too old and too cold to feel warm-blooded passions. He knew only deep waters and shafts of golden light in the shallower turns of the river. He knew only hunger and the satisfaction of that hunger. He knew only this driving instinct that forced him, every few years, to return to the freshwater lakes. Life and death meant nothing to him. He was above such concerns.

And so he wended his way over the many long miles, his great jutting jaws open to receive whatever offerings the river might send him. He ate anything that fit into those jaws, and most things did. But he was not vicious. He was too cold to be vicious. The wide pale eyes, so enormous that they could penetrate the darkness of plunging ocean depths, were devoid of all expression.

He did not realize it, but his sole desire was a single moment to know that he truly lived. This is all any of his kind desire.

For Hydrus that moment was coming.

Ita found her brother on the outskirts of Rannul. This was unusual, for Draven rarely permitted himself to be seen by any of his people, retreating more and more into solitude as the months went by. He wore a beard now, new and sparse but slowly thickening—a testimony to his manhood, however disgraced that manhood might be.

He was hard at work chipping away at a stone, slowly applying his chisel as he sought to craft the most valuable shape. If the carving came out well, it could be turned into a brutal weapon. If his hand slipped or his eye misjudged by even a fraction, well, the stone could still be made into a farming tool. This, however, was considered an ignominious end to a stone-shaper's work, so Draven's whole attention concentrated on each small chip.

Crack went the stone on stone. Then, very gently, a puff of breath to blow away the debris.

Ita waited until after he had blown his breath and before he started his next chip. She balanced on one leg and, when the moment presented itself, gave him a smart tap with her crutch.

"Argh!" Draven gasped, dropping his chisel rather than risk a stray blow. He turned a scowling face up to Ita, his eyes gleaming with the combination of wariness and resentment that had become a permanent fixture since his naming. As he recognized his sister the wariness relaxed though the resentment redoubled. "Ita!" he growled. "Away with you, fool girl. You are standing in my light."

"I am not," said Ita, which was true, for she had shifted from it even as he spoke. "Brother," she said, "put down your stone and come with me."

"Come with you where?" he demanded, taking up his chisel in direct rebellion against his sister's order. "Have you no good labor to which you might turn those idle hands of yours?"

"I do!" she exclaimed. "The best labor, indeed. But I need you and your strong arms."

He pretended to inspect his work in progress, but cast his sister a sideways glance. "Do you mean to say your arms aren't strong enough?" His eyes held a devilish glint, but he flinched, knowing what her response would be, and narrowly avoided a harsh kick from her.

Ita, nearly overbalancing, sank heavily onto the support of her branch. "My arms are strong enough for what I have in mind," she said. "Strong and quick too, quicker than yours! But I cannot steer a canoe and aim a spear at the same time."

This caught Draven's attention enough that he lowered the stone to his lap and turned his head to fully look into his sister's eager face. "Aim a—Ita, what deeds are you plotting in that foolish little head of yours?"

Grunting, Ita sank down into a crouch, bringing her face close to Draven's own. In a voice hushed with mounting excitement she said, "I am going to hunt Hydrus!"

Draven laughed. In retrospect he realized this was taking his life into his hands, for Ita never took kindly to laughter, not if she felt she was being mocked in any way. But he could not help himself. The very idea that his pale, hollow-eyed, club-footed sister would hunt the mighty quarry that had eluded several generations' worth of Rannul's stoutest warriors . . . well, it was too much! So he laughed.

But when he saw the smile twisting the corners of Ita's mouth, the bright light flickering in her eyes, he found his mirth cut short. He cleared his throat, shaking his head at her. "You're mad. Mad as a spring fly."

"They say only the maddest will hunt Hydrus to his end," Ita said. She put out her hand and clutched Draven by the shoulder. "Come with me now!" she urged. "This is his season. He will pass our banks any moment. I have listened carefully to the old men and I have asked them questions. They say when the first red aster blooms and the morning bird sings at dusk, that is the time. Hydrus will come. Brother!" Her grip on his arm tightened, and she would have pulled him to his feet had she possessed the strength. "I saw the first aster this morning, bright as blood in the grass just outside my door! It is a sign. I will hunt Hydrus. I will claim him!"

How many other hopeful hunters had seen the asters and read them as signs? Too many to number, Draven was sure. He himself, only a few years ago, had taken up his spear and, an aster tucked into his hair for luck, gone hunting, desire to bring home the great prize hot in his breast. But it had all been for nothing. Sometimes years would pass with no sign of Hydrus, for he was wily and could pass at night unseen in the darkest deeps of Hanna's flow. Sometimes hunters would claim to have glimpsed him on his journey north and would set traps for his return. But these were never strong enough. No, only a spear could end this hunt, but what good was a spear against quarry one could not see?

"Ita . . ." Draven began, more gently than he'd spoken before. But gentleness was the worst possible approach when it came to his fierce sister.

Ita pushed violently against him and, grimacing with pain, hauled herself upright. Her eyes flashed with anger, and her fist clenched white-knuckled at her side. "I cannot do this on my own," she said. "But if you will not help me, I will still try."

Hearing these familiar words, Draven felt his gut roil. He wondered if she even remembered speaking them in that overgrown field all those months ago. From the look in her eye, she did not. The whole of her being was set upon here and now, the urgency of her own strong will.

"You will fail," Draven said even as he set aside his work and stood, towering over his sister.

She stared up at him, her jaw tight. How like Gaher she looked in that moment, despite the frailty of her features. "I will still try," she repeated.

And so Draven knew that, even as before, his sister would have her way. He would not see her fail. He would not allow it.

Not as he had already failed himself.

Ita insisted that they use Draven's canoe hidden in the culvert, thereby keeping anyone in Rannul from knowing their intent. Draven did not argue, though he knew most of the men were far upriver, gone to inspect a disputed copper mine on the edge of Rannul territory. Rumor spread that the chieftain of Kahorn was sending raiding parties to capture the precious ore. Tensions with Kahorn had redoubled since the prisoner's escape, and it would take less than a rumor to set the war drums sounding. It was only a matter of time.

Draven kept pace with Ita, pretending he didn't have to significantly slow his stride to match hers as they made their way through the rough woodlands along the river's edge toward his secret place. He carried Ita's spear for her, for she found it difficult to navigate the overgrown trails with both crutch and spear. How she expected to balance herself on that clubfoot and hurl her weapon, all without overturning the canoe, Draven could not imagine. But again, he did not ask and he did not argue.

At times his gaze wandered to the forests across the river. They were even more thickly grown than the forests on this side, an effective shield hiding all the Kahorn doings. He wondered again at Callix's enigmatic warning spoken in the dark. And he wondered if the Kahorn prince had survived the trek back to his home village.

They reached the hidden culvert, and Draven went first down the narrow path so that Ita could use his shoulder for support at need. She took hold of him once. He could hear her heavy breathing and knew the trek from the village had sapped her feeble strength. But he did not suggest that they give up the hunt. One glance at her determined face and he knew he did not dare.

His canoe had been much battered during the nighttime ride down the rapids, and he had been obliged to carry it by land back into hiding, for there was no paddling against the river's currents in this place. But it was still solid, and Draven assisted Ita into the front, tucking her spear and a few of his own down the middle, along with a waterskin.

"Be prepared to lean when I tell you," he said.

"Shall I have a paddle?" she asked, and if he didn't know better, he might have suspected he heard a tremor in her voice.

"No," Draven replied. "Hanna provides more than enough power, and I will provide the direction. You must simply keep balance."

Ita nodded. Her eyes were bright with excitement, for she had never gone over the rapids. The rushing waters did not worry Draven now even as he pushed off and felt Hanna catch the canoe in her eager pull. After that nighttime adventure, the rapids gave him not a moment's fear. And he knew Ita would be careful. Her slight weight could hardly make a difference to the balance in any case.

Not once did Ita scream, even during the largest of the swift-moving drops. She held tight to the sides of the canoe, leaning by intuition. Only once did she lean wrong, but Draven compensated by the strength of his arm, and they were never in danger of overturning. Even so, once they were free of the rapids Ita sat for some while, exhausted and unspeaking.

Draven felt guilt sink like a stone in his gut. This was a mistake. He should never have brought her. He should have worked harder to dissuade her. She was mad, and she never would see reason . . .

But suddenly she turned to him, and her eyes were very bright. "They haven't hunted Hydrus down here, beyond the rapids," she said. "I asked the old men, and none of them had. Perhaps their fathers did, but I doubt it. This is where we will find him, brother! I know it."

Draven decided not to mention that he had hunted Hydrus in these waters to no success. Let her have her dream, at least for a while.

He paddled slowly, and Ita climbed up to the very front of the canoe, her eyes intent upon the water. Draven, however, found his gaze drifting more often to the far shore. He saw the high promontory with the single bare tree at its crown. He watched it as they drew near and even as they passed under it, wondering why it had caused the prisoner such fear. For though its rock walls dominated the landscape, Draven could see nothing strange or fearful about it.

The promontory behind them, they continued down the river in silence. Draven began to suspect that Ita would have him proceed forever downriver. But at last, without any reason he could discern, she said, "Here. It will be here."

It was as good a place as any, Draven had to admit. The river came to a small curve in this spot, and though a deep trench ran down the middle, there were shallower patches where the lithe form of Hydrus might, if luck was on their side, be spotted. Draven took the canoe to the bank and moored it so that it would not be pulled further down river. Once the canoe was secure, Ita took up her spear as though she expected Hydrus to appear within moments.

Draven shook his head and settled down for a long wait. The end of this, he knew, would be a return journey up the river, a mooring of the canoe before they reached the rapids, then a long, dark, exhausting trek along the banks. He would have to return for the canoe later, for he suspected he would need to carry his sister part of the way. She would resist, but he knew she would never make that long walk on her own.

He cursed himself for allowing her to talk him into this. But Ita was so strong in spirit, it was easy to forget how frail her body really was.

Suddenly Ita gave a great sigh and relaxed her tense and watchful position, sitting back in the canoe. Draven said nothing but passed the waterskin, from which she drank deeply. Finished, she wiped her mouth and turned to Draven. Tired though they were, a light of mischief flickered deep in her eyes.

"So, dear brother," she said, "how does the fair Lenila these days?"

Draven's face did not alter even by the merest twitching of his cheek. He answered evenly, "I would not know."

"Indeed? I have watched you make lamb's eyes at her since last summer! I'm certain you, of all people, are aware of the comings and goings of Rannul's brightest blossom." Ita smiled teasingly. "She has taken her woman's name now, so a husband must be found for her soon. Do you think—"

"I think Lenila will never take a husband who bears the name Coward," said Draven. Again his face and voice betrayed nothing. But he could not meet his sister's gaze, turning instead to study the placid waters of Hanna.

Ita made no response to this but shifted her weight so that the canoe rocked and water sloshed along its sides. She never called him by his new name—always she said "brother" or, sometimes in a forgetful moment, "Gaho." Never "Draven." It was as though she had washed the memory of his disgrace from her mind.

Or perhaps she did not view his actions as the disgrace they were. This was both a comfort and an irritation to Draven. Much though he valued the unquestioning trust of this one small heart, he could not appreciate his sister's tendency to ignore the reality of his situation.

Ita broke her silence with another great sigh and spoke rather more softly than before. "No man of Rannul would take a wife with a great clubfoot," she said.

But this was no longer the truth, as both Draven and Ita well knew. Since Draven's naming and subsequent fall from grace, Ita's prominence had risen in the village. For now the man to whom Gaher gave her in marriage would become heir to the chiefdom. Ita, who had believed all her life that she would not marry and never fretted in the belief, now fretted indeed, knowing that she would be given to the biggest, bravest, and bloodiest of all her father's warriors. When she received her woman's name, the vying for her hand would begin.

How the currents of their lives had turned. And how unwelcome the turning!

The heaviness of afternoon fell upon them. The sun was bright and golden overhead, without a cloud to mar his view of doings in the mortal world below. But the trees overhanging the bank were shelter enough against his glare, and neither Draven nor Ita suggested moving on or going back. Not yet. An autumnal haze fell upon the both of them. Draven, gazing after the river's flow, felt as though he cast his vision into the water and let it be carried for many leagues away, far away. All the way to the rumored Endless Water where Hydrus dwelt.

Who knew what lands might exist beyond those waves? Or, if no country, what oblivion? Draven could hardly say which idea he preferred.

Suddenly, Ita sat up straight. Her motion startled Draven and rocked the canoe. He looked at her sharply, expecting to see her point out some likely shadow beneath the river's surface. Instead she stared at the bank to which they were moored, and her face had gone pale. "Brother!" she gasped. "Look!"

He looked over his shoulder. And he saw a strange sight indeed.

All along the river's bank, as though rushing silently to this very place where brother and sister waited, a host of brilliantly red asters were opening up their faces, vivid in the light of the descending sun. They gathered thickest near the canoe as though, if they could, they would spread across the surface of the river and grasp hold of it. Draven had never before seen so many of the wild scarlet blooms in one place.

Before he could catch his breath, a certain silvery voice fell upon their ears: the liquid song of a morning thrush in the branches above their heads. Ita stared up into the thick tangle of overshadowing leaves, gold-touched with the beginning of autumn color. She saw the thrush, his head high, his eye bright, his speckled breast swelled with song.

"It's time!" Ita cried, drowning out the melody in her excitement. She stood in the canoe, ignoring both the pain in her foot and the mad rocking that could have overturned them if not for her brother's solid counterweight. "Untie us! Untie us!" she said, reaching for the mooring line with fingers that trembled too hard to be effective.

"Sit down!" Draven barked, and to his surprise, his sister obeyed. He yanked the line free and pushed the canoe back out into the river, using his paddle and the strength of his arm to steady them against the pull of the current. The song of the thrush followed them, but now their senses were much too fixed upon the river itself to pay it heed.

Ita caught up her spear and, ignoring the fiery pain shooting up her leg, stood in the front of the canoe, balancing with far more grace and experience than Draven would have expected. Perhaps she had been practicing without his knowledge.

She raised the spear above her head, grasping the shaft loosely at its balance point. Any pain she experienced was completely lost in the intensity of her focus. Nevertheless, if Hydrus should by some miracle pass this way at this hour, he might easily slip past through the deep trench in the middle of the river. It would take a stroke of luck unimaginable—

Ita did not have to speak a word. Draven saw the excitement shoot through her body, and he followed her gaze to see, to his utmost surprise, the dark ribbon just beneath the water's surface. It could be any of the great fish, a smaller mate of Hydrus's perhaps. But he knew this wasn't so. Not with the morning bird singing at sunfall.

Ita shifted just a little, enough to communicate everything required to her brother. With a dip of his paddle he turned the canoe, presenting Ita with the best and broadest view of the approaching fish.

And then he was near.

Hydrus!

Hydrus was near!

The dream of every warrior. The magnificent, the cold and ancient one. The setting sun's rays glanced off the river, but not here. No glare was cast just here.

They beheld enormous eyes meant for seeing in the darkest places. His jutting lower jaw boasted no teeth but was sharp and deadly like that of some weirdly misshapen snapping turtle, open to catch anything that might swim too near. Trailing dorsal fins crowned his head; ten long rays, one for each decade of his life. The pelvic fins were similarly elongated, red-tipped and trailing down the length of his long body. It would have been impossible to say, in that heart-thudding moment, just how long that body was. Fifteen, even eighteen rods of twisting, writhing power. The body was scaleless, the black skin covered with a silvery guanine.

He was hideous. He was beautiful.

He was near.

For an instant, a certain future flashed through Draven's mind. He saw it all. He saw himself plunging his paddle hard and turning the canoe, putting Ita off balance so that her aim went wide. He saw himself preventing what he knew must happen—preventing the success of his proud, brave sister. Preventing her from capturing the heart's dream of every man in Rannul. He saw this dark vision, and for the time it took his heart to pound in a single beat, he considered.

Instead, Draven held the canoe firm. All was silent in the ears of both brother and sister poised in this too-brief moment. They did not hear the song of the morning bird. They did not hear the murmur of the river. They did not hear the sudden stilling of the wind that might have blown Ita's spear off course. Their ears were deaf. Their sight was all.

Ita drew back her arm and threw.

The force with which she hurled her spear caused her to lose all balance. Draven had not even the chance to cry out before his sister disappeared beneath the river's surface. His ears, still deaf, did not even hear the splash.

And Ita plunged down, down. She felt the pull of the current and knew suddenly, with a heave of her heart, the great strength of Hydrus, who swam against that pull with ease. She forced her eyes open, though the water was too dark for vision.

Yet she did see. Perhaps she only imagined it. Nevertheless, she saw.

She saw the great eye of Hydrus fixed upon her with cold clarity. She saw the body writhe and turn its massive, ugly, snapping jaws. She saw the blood where her spear, thrown true, had pierced the mighty fish. Then another twist, and Hydrus gazed at her again.

For a moment they looked upon one another—the girl who felt every pain, every shame, to the fullest depths of her heart; the fish who felt nothing, who never had felt anything, who moved only according to instinct.

They were one. They looked into each other's eyes, and ever so briefly both knew, in a moment of conjoined wonder, the wholeness, the truth of life.

Then Hydrus's massive, twisting body wrapped around Ita. The long rays of his pelvic fins lashed at her face and hands, burning with sharpness she did not expect. The weight of him was crushing, and she had not the strength to break free. But all was well, even in pain: She would die with him gladly for the sake of having lived such a moment.

Just as her lungs were ready to give up and her heart ready to give out, she felt Hydrus's body pulled away. Powerful arms closed around her, and the next thing she knew, her head broke the surface of the river. Her ears worked again, and she heard the voice of Hanna and choruses of the forest shouting, perhaps in outrage, perhaps in encouragement. It hardly mattered. She heard her brother's voice in her ear saying, "Relax. Don't fight me."

She obeyed, and Draven bore her safely to shore. Her sodden clothes weighed heavily upon her, and she could scarcely raise herself up enough to cough and gasp for breath. She wanted to collapse and lie there upon the bank forever.

But she raised her head, crying, "Hydrus!"

She needn't have worried. The moment he'd safely deposited her on the shore, Draven plunged back into the river, allowing the current to carry him swiftly. Ita sat up, pushing wet hair from her eyes, and saw the enormous, twisting body caught in the shallow bend of the river. Any moment now, Hanna would catch it up and bear it away forever.

But Draven reached it and hauled it to the shore. It was so vast, she could see his every muscle straining. He could not get it all the way onto the riverbank but managed to haul at least half of it up before he collapsed, exhausted by the effort.

And so they lay—brother, sister, and mighty Hydrus—as the sun fell behind the trees.

Ita's trophy was far too big to carry back to Rannul. Ita could not even carry herself. She had abused her foot too much for one day, and she would not walk for many hours yet. But she refused to leave her trophy behind.

"No!" she insisted when Draven reached out to pick her up. "No, I will stay. I will guard Hydrus and I will sing the songs of death and passing over him. You go to Rannul, as fast as you can, and tell our father what we have done. They will come. They will help."

She could not see the strange, sorrowful look on Draven's face, for dusk was too heavy on the world, and her eyes were too full of Hydrus's vastness to notice anything else.

Draven did not argue. He looked up and down the river, wishing he might spot his canoe come to ground somewhere near so that he might fetch the remaining spears and leave his sister a weapon at least. "If something should come upon you in the darkness—" he began.

"It will see what I have done and turn away in fear!" Ita replied fiercely, though she herself could not even stand.

So Draven took a small stone knife from his belt and placed it in her hands. He kissed the top of her head before turning and darting into the forest, making his way with all speed back up the riverbank.

How long she sat there keeping watch over Hydrus, Ita never could say. She sang the songs of passing in time to the river's murmur, her hand lightly touching the slimy head of the fish as she sang. Her arms and face still burned with the cuts he had given her, but she did not blame him for that. Indeed, she welcomed the pain as her just reward. Hydrus's eyes were as wide and staring in death as ever they were in life. An eerie companion was he, and yet Ita would not have traded this long, lonely vigil for anything.

Once she thought she heard the morning bird sing again, its silver voice beckoning to her. She raised her head and gazed about, seeking after the little singer. She found herself looking across the river.

What was that she saw? On the far bank, in moonlight . . . Who was that standing with a weapon in hand, as though on guard? A form too far away to recognize, and yet somehow familiar. A stranger, an enemy even, on the enemy's shore.

And yet it seemed to Ita that her eyes met his across the darkness, across the water. Had he seen her fight with Hydrus? Though it may have been a trick of the moonlight, she thought he raised his spear in salute.

But the sudden sound of approaching drums drew her gaze away. Ita turned to look up the bank and saw torchlight. The men of Rannul approached. Casting a glance back across the water, Ita sought the watchful form of the stranger. But he was gone, whoever he was, and her heart sank in that knowledge.

Then the drums were all around her, and the torchlight shone upon the faces of her father and his proudest warriors.

"What, Ita?" cried Gaher, swooping down upon her and catching her up in his arms. "What is it you have done, my fierce wolf pup?" And he grinned hugely as he surveyed the vast coils of Hydrus's body. The warriors splashed into the river, and it took sixteen of them to lift that great trophy up onto their shoulders. Several cried out with surprise as Hydrus's fins cut their hands.

"My daughter has done this!" Gaher declared, his eyes bright in his bearded face. "My Ita. My *Itala!*" He declared her woman's name with pride, and his daughter's heart beat fast with a mixture of joy and sudden terror at the enormity of adulthood come down upon her shoulders.

So the sixteen warriors carried Hydrus back to the village, drums beating and voices shouting victory songs all the way. Gaher and another of his men bore Ita up on their shoulders, and she was obliged to duck and push branches away, so quickly did they carry her back to the victory feasting of Rannul. She longed for nothing so much as to crawl into her small sod house and sleep for days. But this could not be. For she had conquered a dream.

All through the night and the long day following, she cast about for some glimpse of Draven. But she did not see him, not for a seven-night following.

MORTAL SORROW

T HE OLD WOMAN sat silently for such a long time after finishing her tale, the girl began to wonder if her grandmother had gone to sleep with her eyes open. She seemed to gaze up at the carving of Draven, but her heart and mind were a hundred leagues away.

At length she blinked and addressed herself to Akilun, asking quietly, "Did I tell it right? Is that how the story goes?"

"Indeed you told it perfectly," Akilun assured her. He had not worked on his carving but stood and listened to the whole of the tale without once moving or interrupting. "I could not have told it better myself." Then he turned to the girl and smiled at her, and she flushed with pleasure, though her shyness made her lean into her grandmother.

"And what do you make of such a tale?" Akilun asked her.

"I want to spear a big fish," the girl replied promptly.

To her dismay, both Grandmother and Akilun laughed. Her flush deepened, this time with embarrassment. "Are there no more big fish like Hydrus?" she asked. She could not remember seeing any among the fishermen's catches, though her fearful imagination had sometimes glimpsed dark shadows slipping beneath the river's surface, which made her hesitant to wade out very far.

"Not so big, no," her grandmother told her, still chuckling softly. "But I am sure Hydrus has many grandsons who will, in time, equal him in length and might. Perhaps we will spy one someday soon? After all, Hydrus himself was hunted so very long ago."

The girl nodded at this, and though she shivered at the idea of such a monster in her own dear river, it was a delicious shiver. For the first time she felt what a delight fear might be. "I shall have to practice my throwing arm."

"Yes," her grandmother agreed and rose stiffly from her seat, grimacing at the pain and pressing a hand to her hip. But she changed the grimace into another smile and leaned on the girl's thin shoulder. "We must go now. You may practice your throwing arm this very day and perhaps spear us something to add to the cooking fires tonight. Something smaller than Hydrus."

Akilun escorted them to the door of the Great House and even across the work yard. At the beginning of the forest path he bowed respectfully to Grandmother, once more making the reverent signs, to which she responded in like kind. Then, narrowing her eyes as she studied him, Grandmother asked, "Will you tell her the whole of the story?"

"Do you wish it, good lady?" Akilun asked.

"I do," said she. "It is a hard tale. But it is time that she knew it, and

I would have her hear it from you."

"In that case, I will tell her." Akilun made another bow which seemed to include the girl. This delighted her. She was not one to receive such courteous gestures, not a scrawny child like she!

The girl was thoughtful as she supported her grandmother back down the hillside. Her mind was full of the river and the rushing water and the mighty twists and churnings of Hydrus. But she found herself considering more thoughtfully the end of the tale and those things her grandmother had spoken of then.

"I think I know how the story will go," she said before they'd even come in sight of the village.

"Do you, now?" said her grandmother, the first she'd spoken since leaving Akilun's presence. Her voice was tired. The journey up the hillside really was too long for her these days, and she limped painfully. "Then you must certainly return and hear the rest, for how else will you know if you guessed rightly?"

The girl nodded at the wisdom of this, determined to carry the waterskin up to the Great House again.

It was late in the afternoon the following day before the girl found a chance to snatch up the waterskin and hasten up the hillside. Summer was at its height, and there was much work to be done about Kallias village, preparing for the long winter while there was still time. The storehouses must be filled to brimming with all manner of dried fishes and mushrooms and smoked meats.

The girl had spent much of the day brushing mushrooms as clean as she could with a brush made of stiff grasses. She could not wash them with water, for then they would waterlog and not dry properly. Once they were clean, she cut them into pieces and spread them out to dry on a high, hot stone, guarding them from flies and thieving squirrels. It wasn't difficult work—indeed, it was rather boring. But it took quite a lot of time.

At last, however, she caught her mother's skirts as Iulia hastened by. "Have we delivered the water gift today?" the girl asked.

"Oh, great airy gods!" Iulia cried, her gaze turning up to the promontory. Then she helped her daughter to her feet and gave her a push in the right direction. "Do it for me now, won't you, child? You can fill the skin yourself. And hurry!"

Delighted, the girl hastened to obey and was soon well on her way up the track to the Great House. Already the sky was beginning to turn gold, and the forest around her wore a thick, lazy aspect. The girl, by contrast, was excited and alert, eager to tell Akilun her guesses about his story.

The courtyard had changed dramatically since the day before. Indeed, when she stepped from the trees, the girl half wondered if she'd somehow taken a wrong turn and come to a new world entirely. For the work yard was no longer cluttered with stone debris, discarded tools, and bits of dismantled scaffolding. All of this had been swept away as though by some magic and the dirt ground beneath laid with astoundingly smooth and flat blocks of stone. It looked like ice to the girl, and she stepped onto it with great wariness, afraid her feet would slip. It was solid, though gleaming and bright.

Moving cautiously, the girl approached the Great House. She could hear a hammer pounding far away; only one, if her ears told her correctly. Probably the Strong One, hard at work, as always. But where then was the Kind One? She searched around the Great House, afraid to call out for fear of attracting the Strong One's notice, but did not see Akilun anywhere.

At last she was obliged to approach the great door and peer into the depths of the hall. She found, when she did so, that the huge empty space inside no longer frightened her as much as it had. If she spent too much time peering into the deeper shadows, her courage would surely fail her. But instead her eyes instinctively sought the glimmering light of Akilun's lantern. She saw it and the form of Akilun himself sitting before the carving.

The girl slipped through the doors, clutching the waterskin tightly, then crossed the hall and made her way up behind Akilun. The statue had changed since yesterday too. Now most of the shoulders and upper torso were in place, and all of one arm. The other arm, which seemed to be lifting something up, was unfinished. She wondered if it would hold a weapon when Akilun's work was through.

"Is that you, Iulia's daughter?" Akilun asked without looking around.

"Yes," the girl replied, never stopping to wonder how he had known. "I brought your water gift."

"Thank you." But Akilun did not turn to accept the proffered gift. He remained where he sat, his elbows on his knees, gazing up at the carving, his own work. The girl stood for a silent moment then joined him on the floor, sitting cross-legged with the waterskin in her lap. She studied the statue and the new additions, the folds of Draven's shirt and the fur of his cloak.

Then she turned and studied the side of Akilun's face. To her surprise, it was full of deep sorrow.

As though guessing at her unspoken question, Akilun spoke in a low voice: "It is such a strange and sad mystery to me. The mystery of mortality. Even now, so many ages since I first entered this world, I struggle to understand. But I think . . . I think it may be the most beautiful mystery. And those who live within the confines of mortality may perhaps best understand the glory of eternity when it is finally revealed.

Nevertheless, it is strange. And so sad."

The girl didn't understand any of this. Akilun spoke in his own language, and the words could not take full shape in her mind, instead leaving only vague impressions of sound and color, like the end of a long rain shower, the distant rumble of retreating thunder, and the first ray of sunlight bursting through the gloom.

The girl shrugged and rested her chin in her hands. "I think I know what will happen in the story," she said.

"Is that so?" Akilun glanced down at her, one eyebrow upraised.

"Yes. Ita—Itala, rather—will fall in love with the prisoner. The prince across the river. That's how stories go. Good stories, that is. And they must marry at the end."

Akilun smiled at this speculation, and it was not a mocking smile. "Perhaps," he said, nodding. "Before this ending you suggest may come to pass, however, there are many impediments for them to surmount. You see, not long after Itala hunted Hydrus, winter fell, and the world was frozen and quiet for many long months. But when at last the snows melted and the ground thawed once more, Gaher bade the war drums sound . . ."

OF BLOOD
AND MADNESS

T HE WARRIORS OF RANNUL marched down to the river, where they soon filled the canoes to brimming. All the village gathered at the water's edge to see them off. Barefoot children screeched small variations on the deep-throated battle cries of their fathers and older brothers. Women said many prayers to the uncaring gods of the air and sky, but their eyes were bright with pride as well as sorrow.

Draven and Itala stood side by side a little apart from the rest. Itala should have been in the very midst of the gathering, wearing the necklace of bear claws and hawk talons that marked her precedence among the women of Rannul. Instead she remained at her brother's side, watching with him, as solemn-eyed as he. She watched in particular the strong young warrior who climbed into Gaher's own canoe. Oson was his name, and he was the favorite among those who vied for Itala's hand in marriage. If he proved himself as worthy in war as he had proven himself in the hunt, he would become her husband.

Itala lifted her hand to finger the necklace she wore instead of the bear claws. It was much smaller, made of stone-hammered copper flakes in various shapes, strung on a stout gut cord. She shuddered and took some of the weight off of her crutch to lean against the supporting bulk of her brother instead. Draven did not seem to notice. His gaze was fixed upon the far shore where even now the first of the warriors beached their canoes and dragged them up to hide in the foliage.

He should be among them. He should be even now bearing his sickle blade into the thick of that forest, plunging headlong into battle against those wicked Kahorns who plundered Rannul mines, poached Rannul game, and otherwise encroached upon all that by right of ancient conquest belonged to Rannul. He should be whetting his appetite for blood.

Instead his stomach clenched with a mixture of self-reproach and sickening fear. How he hated the peaceful heart in his breast, the heart which loathed the very idea of shedding a man's blood! What a fool. What a coward. What a disgrace to his father's name.

Though he knew he should not, Draven allowed his travelling gaze to rest on the face of lovely Lenila, who stood in the shallows near the riverbank to wave the warriors on. Her pride in her brother, Oson, was evident to all. She never once looked Draven's way.

Draven drew a deep breath and let it out slowly so as not to make a sound. He did not want to call Itala's attention to his sighing. Once more he gazed across the river to where his father's canoe even now rested. He remembered suddenly something he had all but forgotten over the cold winter—the words of the Kahorn prince on the dark shore beyond the promontory.

"*You must not let them cross the river. If they do, they will suffer the same fate as Kahorn.*"

But what fate was that? Little enough had been seen of the tribe across the river, despite all the vicious rumors of plundering war parties. Indeed, Draven suspected that all Gaher's rousing speeches against the many evils of their neighbors were so much vaporous breath upon the wind. So what then had become of Kahorn? And what of the wounded prince?

A sudden gasp from his sister startled Draven from these thoughts. He caught her in his arms even as her knees gave out, and she pressed her face into his chest. He wondered briefly if she was fainting or ill. Then, much to his surprise, he heard a muffled sob.

"Ita!" he exclaimed, speaking her child's name in his anxiety for her. "Ita, sister, what is wrong? Why do you weep?"

But Itala—his brave sister, the slayer of Hydrus, her father's pride—only shook her head. Her tears continued to fall until long after the last warriors disappeared into the shadowy forests of Kahorn country.

Two days later, those who waited in Rannul saw smoke rising across the river. It was distant . . . if the day had not been so clear, they might not have seen it at all.

Draven worked silently, out of sight of the village during this time. He wanted no one to be visibly reminded of his disgrace, of the ugly truth that he was not welcome to march into battle beside his father. So he spent his days hunting, fishing, avoiding the fields and pastures where women and children might glimpse him and throw stones his way. Whatever he successfully caught he delivered to Itala, who in turn delivered it to the rest of the tribe. So he contributed his meager portion, outcast though he was.

He saw the smoke from a quiet inlet of the river where he stood poised to spear. He could not have said what sense drove him to raise his intense gaze from the water where the trout swam to the heavens where the smoke curled. But something moved inside him, and he looked, and he saw. And he wondered.

To whom went the day? Would the warriors of Rannul march home triumphant, their enemies slaughtered?

Would that be a victory?

The face of the prisoner he had refused to kill flashed before his mind's eye. But he shook this thought away and all thoughts of the blood even now being shed, focusing instead on the task at hand.

A week later, the first of the children came running into Rannul village shouting that they'd heard the victory drums beat across the river. Itala, who sat in a quiet place carding lambs' wool, looked up at the sound of the bright, eager voices. Anyone watching her would have seen her face, already pale, turn a ghastly grey. But she set her jaw, put aside her work, and painfully hauled herself up onto her crutch. She could not bring herself to follow the other women down to the river but stood in the village center.

How long she stood there counting her breaths, she did not know. Too soon she heard the victory drums of which the children had spoken. They were expressive drums, speaking of many things in a language of deep reverberations. She knew before she saw the warriors that they returned from a mighty triumph. She knew that Gaher was lauded among his warriors as a great chieftain, slayer of many men. And women. And children too, Itala did not doubt.

She grimaced at a sudden heaving in her gut, wishing to be sick. But she dared not. Someone might see. Someone might see her doubled up in weakness, and this she could never allow. No, for she was the slayer of Hydrus, the pride of Gaher. She must stand strong and greet the warriors. She looked for Draven but did not see him. Then the drums entered the village.

Children swarmed ahead, singing and dancing even as the bloodstained men progressed down the center path between sod houses, Gaher at their head. Itala saw Oson at his right hand and knew what that meant for her future. Once more she felt her stomach heave, for Oson's beard was brown with bloodstains. The champion of Rannul, no doubt. A worthy husband.

Itala steeled her face so that no expression could move it, neither smile nor frown nor grimace. When her father saw her and raised an arm in greeting, she inclined her head respectfully, her hand over her heart. She felt the copper under her fingertips and clutched it momentarily for strength.

But then her father was beside her, a massive arm around her shoulders. "My brave Itala!" he cried. "We are victorious." Then he turned to the gathered tribe and raised his axe above his head. "The Kahorn barbarians will pillage from us no more! Their farms are razed, the village of their chieftain laid low. Those among them yet living are scattered to the four winds! Rannul is safe again."

And all the village set up a great cheer. No one saw how hard Itala clenched her jaw, forcing back the many words that sought to burst from her throat. No one noticed the pallor of her cheek, or if they did, they saw no difference from her usual sallow complexion. After all, though her heart was brave and strong, Itala was weak in body.

"Now where is Oson?" Gaher demanded, and he drew the bloody young man to his side. Oson grinned down at Itala, his eyes full of possessiveness and other things Itala dared not name. The stink of death was on him, and Itala yearned to throw away her crutch and flee through the throng, flee into the forest, into hiding. To disappear like Draven did.

But Itala was no coward. She met Oson's gaze, and her eyes revealed nothing, though the tension in her neck may have revealed much to an observant man.

Oson was not such a man. He laughed and boldly declared his triumphs to her, there in the hearing of all. He spoke of his many kills over the last few days, claiming feats of slaughter unparalleled. Most of his stories were lies, Itala knew. But behind the lies were vicious, brutal truths.

"You see, my fierce little wolf pup?" Gaher said, interrupting Oson in the middle of his declamations. "You see what a fine husband I have found for you? By his strength and your courage, we will see such offspring of my household as will dominate all this region, aye, from here to the Endless Water!"

Another cheer went up. What a fine thing it was to the people of Rannul. Victory over their enemies; a marriage of their princess to a worthy warrior. A feast must be held in short order, the storehouses opened to celebrate such doings.

So Itala found herself caught between her father and her betrothed. Someone found the necklace of bear claws and draped it around her neck, covering up the smaller, more delicate copper necklace. Someone else wrapped her in a heavy cloak, though the spring was already warm and she did not need it. It was ceremonial, however, so she dared not shrug it off. Gaher and Oson also wore fine cloaks over their dirty, gore-spattered bodies, and she nearly gagged many times over at their stench—she, who was used to the slaughtering of livestock and fowl, to skinning and tanning and all manner of odorous perfumes. But this was not the same. She thought she might smother and die in this reek. And through it all, though she sought Draven in the crowd, she did not see him.

Draven remained on the outskirts of the village, watching all the comings and goings, but daring not take part. He saw Itala in the center and Oson seated in the place of honor that should have been his. Lenila hastened to serve the men, laughing and joking and singing by turns.

Had he been a true man, he could have taken part in all of this. If he had spilled the blood when it was ready and warm for offering.

He wondered now if Callix had survived the last few days. Had Draven spared him all those months ago only for the Kahorn prince to fall prey now to another Rannul blade? What purpose would that serve? None Draven could see. And his own life ruined for it!

These dark thoughts and more roiled in his head. Indeed, he hardly knew himself for self-reproach and despair. Then and there he might have sunk into blackness inescapable, had not an evil still more dire set upon the night.

For Oson stood up suddenly. All eyes turned to him, expecting the soon-to-be bridegroom to offer a speech, some praise to his great chief, some lewd compliment to his pale bride. His mouth was open, ready to speak.

Instead he gave a choking, gurgling gasp. No other sound did he make, but fell upon the ground and writhed. His feet lashed out in terrible kicks, striking Itala. She screamed in pain, unable to move quickly enough to get out of his reach. But Gaher rose up and pulled her away, holding her protectively even as he shouted down at the convulsing young warrior. "Oson! What is this devilry? Have you taken too much drink?"

But Oson continued to thrash, and white foam filled his mouth. Women screamed. Lenila, his sister, dropped her serving platter and tried to rush to her brother's side, only to be caught and held back by the other women. So Oson struggled alone in the center of the village, his body weirdly shadowed in the firelight, every muscle straining and shaking.

Then he lay still, save for the swift rise and fall of his chest. He was yet alive. His eyes were wide, staring, unseeing.

"Oson?" Gaher let go of his daughter and crouched before the young man. "Oson, do you hear me?"

But other than his heavy breathing, which Draven could hear even from where he stood in the shadows, Oson gave no sign of life. Even when Gaher touched him, he did not move.

Gaher sat back, looking around at his people, searching the eyes of the old men and women for some knowledge he did not himself possess. He said, "What can this madness be—"

But his voice cut off abruptly when Oson began once more to convulse. This time his agony was worse than before, and women screamed and hid their faces, unwilling to watch such evil doings.

When at last Oson lay still again, Gaher barked orders to his men. "Come! Help me!" he demanded. They came, however unwillingly, gathered up the brawny warrior between them, and bore him away to his own sod house.

For three days Oson lay in darkness, untended save by Lenila and a few others who dared enter his house. The village waited in terror to learn his fate. Questions abounded without answers. Was he bitten by some rabid beast while traveling through Kahorn territory? Had some tribal magician set a curse upon his head?

Draven did not try to see Itala during that time. He remained out of sight, afraid that if he reminded anyone of his presence, they would lay the blame of Oson's sickness at his door. After all, Draven should have been the one marching at his father's side. He should have been the one struck down. Or perhaps no curse could have fallen had the chieftain's son not disgraced himself in the light of dawn. It was hard to understand the ways and wiles of the airy gods.

But Draven alone had heard the warning, the words of Prince Callix: "*You must not let them cross the river . . .*"

At sunfall on the third day the first of the mourners began the death songs, and Draven knew that Oson had died of his mysterious malady. Funeral preparations began; a canoe was prepared to carry the young warrior on his last voyage down the river, perhaps even to the Endless Water.

While all this took place, Draven stole quietly to Oson's house. The body lay alone within. None would sit with the dead man for fear of what evil his unsettled ghost might work. Not even fair Lenila dared draw near but keened her mourning songs far from that dark door. Draven slipped inside and struck a light, holding up a burning rush so that he might look more closely upon the dead man.

Oson was scarcely older than Draven himself. They had been friends once, back when they were only Gaho and Oso, boys playing at war. Since Draven's naming they had not spoken.

Draven crouched before the body, searching for . . . he knew not what. On a sudden impulse he lifted Oson's beard. It was not yet very long or very thick, just enough to cover most of his neck. So Draven lifted it and held the rush light close to see what he might find.

Wrapped around Oson's throat were ten finger-shaped bruises.

TOO DARK
TO SPEAK

A KILUN BROKE OFF HIS story so abruptly, the girl gasped for breath. "What happened next?" she asked, her eyes round with wondering horror.

"No," Akilun said, shaking his head and glancing toward the long windows and the slits of ruddy sunlight cast on the eastern wall. "No, it is too late, too near nightrise to speak of such dark things." He had sat beside the girl throughout this part of his long story, but he stood now and offered a hand to help her stand as well. "Soon," he said, "this House will be full of light, and all things may be spoken of without fear. But for now, let this tale wait until the morrow and the sun's early light."

The girl wanted to argue. Her heart beat a frantic pace following the revelation of what Draven had seen. But she picked up her still-full water skin obediently and allowed herself to be escorted back through the shadowy hall. To her surprise, Akilun continued beside her out the door, down the steps, and across the stone-paved yard.

"What of . . . what of the Strong One?" the girl asked. "Does he not need the water gift?"

But Akilun, his eye on the dusk-deepening sky, shook his head. "Only bring it again earlier tomorrow, and that will be enough for the both of us."

She expected him to part ways with her at the beginning of the downward trail. Instead, Akilun walked beside her all the long way down from the promontory's crest. She was glad, for, caught up as she had been in his story, she had not realized how old the day had grown. Indeed, the moon already rose into purpling clouds, and the sun had fallen almost beyond view. The people of Kallias would be drawing near to the nighttime fires, and meals would be cooking over hot coals. The girl had never before been out so late. She felt that she should be more frightened by the dark whispers of the surrounding forest, but her mind was so full of the story she had just heard, she found no time for such childish fears.

Before they came quite within sight of the village, Akilun stopped. "You go on from here," he told her. "I will stand by until I know you are safe."

How he would know, the girl could not guess. Perhaps he could see farther than she could. However it was, she made a quick sign of reverence then hastened on her way, still holding the waterskin tightly. She hoped her mother would not notice that it was still full and ask why the water gift had not been delivered.

She felt Akilun's eyes on her until she stepped within the village borders. There she turned around, wondering if she could catch a glimpse of him up the hillside track. But she saw nothing. Still she knew that he was there, watching over her until she was safely home.

The girl did not wait for her mother to send her up the hill the following day. As soon as the morning was well progressed, she snatched up the waterskin, emptying it of yesterday's untasted water as she raced down to the river to fill it afresh. Then she darted back up to the village, found her mother, and said, "The Kind One—Akilun—he asked me to bring the gift early today."

"Oh?" Iulia looked up from the grain she ground with stone and mortar, shading her eyes to study her daughter. "Well, if that is so—"

"It is so, Mother! I must go at once."

Iulia frowned, ready to protest. But before she could form the words, her own mother hobbled from the hut behind her, laughing and saying, "You can see the girl is ready to flit away like a swallow! Best let her go before she strains her wings."

Iulia glanced between her old mother and her young daughter, perhaps guessing at some secret understanding between the two to which she was not privy. With a shrug and a wave of her hand, she said, "Go on then."

And the girl, with a swift smile of thanks to her grandmother, was away up to the Great House once more.

She found Akilun once more at work on his carving. Between Akilun and his brother, they seemed to make miraculous progress on all the enormous tasks involved in raising such a House—stone carving, floor laying, mortar and measurements, things she could not begin to comprehend. Yet, in comparison to the wonders they worked all around, Akilun's progress on this one carving was painfully slow.

Draven's upraised arm was more defined than it had been the day before, but his hand and whatever he was holding aloft remained formless. More and more the original shape of the ugly stump disappeared, giving way to cloak and torso and strong legs. But always Draven's face drew the girl's gaze, so noble did it seem to her in the light of Akilun's lantern.

Akilun himself crouched, working on what looked like the beginnings of Draven's right foot. Though he did not look around, he called out to the girl in greeting, saying, "So you have come early, have you?"

The girl did not respond to this. She crossed the cavernous hall, not even noticing how little now she feared its vastness, and sat down just within the circle of lantern light, the waterskin propped up beside her. "I've been thinking," she said, "about the story. I still believe what I said yesterday is true. I believe Itala loves the prisoner, Callix. He gave her the copper necklace, didn't he?"

Akilun glanced her way, a smile on his mouth though his hands continued to work the chisel, paring away the wood in thin, gentle curls. "Are you so very certain that is how the story must go?"

"Yes. It must," the girl insisted, though how she had come to this conclusion she could not say. Yet when Akilun did not immediately respond, she felt a sliver of doubt slip into her heart. "Am I not right?" she asked.

"You may be, Iulia's daughter," Akilun replied.

"But what became of him then? Was he killed? What of the tribe across the river, the Kahorn people?"

"Patience," said Akilun. *Tap, tap, tap* went his hammer and chisel. "Patience, and I will tell you how it went."

BLACKENED EMBERS

PERHAPS WE DESERVE IT. All of us.

It had been easy to think otherwise at first when it was just Oson who was taken. Itala had hidden in the young women's house, her crutch beside her, her legs drawn up to her chest, and she had prayed to all the airy gods she could name that Oson would not survive whatever strange malady had taken him. That he—her brutal, bloody intended—would follow into death all those he had slain, and she would be free of him.

It was probably a sin to pray such prayers. The gods did not seem to hear her one way or the other, so she doubted it mattered. And when one of the village maids carried word to her that Oson had died, Itala did not give thanks. She merely nodded and, when the maid had gone, bowed her head and clutched the copper necklace close to her heart. Even when she heard Lenila's mourning songs rising up into the dark of evening, Itala felt no surge of pity. The world was a better place free of such a beast.

But before dawn the next day another victim fell down convulsing, foaming at the mouth—an old warrior with grey in his beard who had survived his share of campaigns and cruel winters. He was dead in two days.

Panic spread through Rannul. Rumors of mad dogs spread, and many loyal beasts were slain in fear. It did no good. For scarcely had the old warrior's funeral canoe been launched in swift pursuit of Oson's then another man fell prey to the same sickness, this one a grandfather long past his fighting years.

And when the grandfather died, Accata, a mother of three grown sons, was next.

Itala stood outside Accata's house, leaning heavily on her crutch and listening to the hushed murmurs of the one old medicine woman who dared tend the sick. The murmurs were healing chants spoken with earnest belief. But similar prayers had done no good three times already. Why should these be any different?

"Perhaps we deserve it," Itala whispered. A cold spring wind bearing the memory of winter caught in her hair and bit her cheeks. "Even Accata. For she is the mother of killers."

A spasm of pain up her leg made her grimace. Her clubfoot hurt for no reason sometimes, even when she took extra care to put no pressure on it. She cursed bitterly but then swallowed the curses back. After all, if Accata deserved this frightening illness then surely Itala deserved all her pains. She may not have birthed killers yet. But she was the daughter of a killer, born of a proud line of killers. Indeed, had her soul been switched for her brother's at birth—had she been born with the strong man's body he boasted instead of this crippled frame in which her spirit was housed—she had no doubt that she would have marched into battle alongside Gaher. For did she not crave the acclaim of her people as much as any man?

Had she not slain Hydrus?

She turned then and hobbled away from Accata's house, moving slowly and painfully out of the village, down to the river. She progressed through the trees, ignoring the pain, panting sharp breaths through gritted teeth. Many times she was obliged to stop and rest herself but never for long. After all, she had much farther to go this time and could allow for no weakness. Let her body fail her later . . . but not now. Not now.

At last she stood above Draven's secret culvert, her gaze following the fall of the many thin streams. The river was loud here, and it was difficult to hear much else. But Itala believed her ears discerned a tapping of stone on stone.

"Brother!" she cried. "Are you there?"

She was obliged to cry out three times before he heard her. Then Draven stepped away from the wall and into her line of vision. His beard had grown in during the last many months—still a young man's beard but covering the whole lower half of his face. He would never allow it to grow long like a warrior's, for he had not earned that right. Even so, he looked much older than he had a year ago.

"Itala, go home," he said.

But she shook her head and started down the narrow trail. She knew this would bring him up in a hurry. Sure enough, he was scrambling up beside her within moments. "What are you doing here?" he demanded, his voice heavy with weariness. "You should not seek me out."

"Oh, and I should remain in the village listening to mourners wail instead?" she demanded. "Are you the only one permitted to hide?"

He bowed his head, and she thought perhaps he felt shame for abandoning her in the village. But when he looked up again, there was such a stricken expression in his face, she felt her anger at him dissipate.

"Have you not wondered," he asked so quietly that she scarcely heard him over Hanna's roar, "if I am the cause of Rannul's suffering?"

"Never," Itala said immediately, perhaps too quickly for belief. But she reached out and took his arm, gazing at him earnestly. "Rannul's suffering is Rannul's own fault. Not yours, my brother—or no more than any other man's. After all, you did not march into war against those who could not defend themselves."

Here Draven frowned. "Could not defend themselves? What do you mean by this? Has not Kahorn always been our deadly enemy? Have we not striven against them for many generations?"

"Maybe. I don't know," Itala replied. "But I do know that Kahorn was unprepared for such an attack. I do know they could do nothing as the warriors of Rannul set upon them."

"How could you know this?"

"Callix told me."

The next moment Itala found herself pouring out the whole of her story. Draven's face was stony, devoid of expression, but she did not care. She had carried this secret so long, and her heart hurt with the need to tell someone of her hidden fears and hidden pain.

"He came to see me soon after we hunted Hydrus," she said. She always said "we" when she spoke of that hunt, though among the people of Rannul no acknowledgement of Draven's part was ever made. "He brought me a gift. A gift his father once gave to his mother." She drew the copper necklace out from under her garments, and it caught the sunlight gently. "He said that his mother told him to give it to the bravest woman he met, and with it, to give his heart. He told me that he had never seen a braver woman."

Her voice caught, but she drew a deep breath and forced herself to continue. "He thanked me for my part in saving his life and said that throughout his whole long march back home he thought of me. I don't think he ever saw my—my evil foot or this crutch I must carry. He saw only my heart, and he thought it fine and valiant. So he gave me this necklace, and he told me that he would never forget me."

Draven said nothing. He scarcely moved.

"He came again, a few times only," Itala continued. "It is so dangerous for him to enter our territory. He knows what our father would do to him if he is caught. But he came anyway and . . . and I . . ." She clutched the necklace in her fist. "Brother, I think he must be dead. Our father claims Kahorn village was destroyed. Callix would have fought in its defense. And I need to know . . ."

She could say no more. She could only meet her brother's unreadable gaze, and it was the bravest thing she had ever done. Indeed, as Draven studied his sister's face, he saw there for the first time the true depths of the fear she was capable of feeling. And he saw her struggle to surmount that fear, and he knew that she was courageous indeed.

He said nothing of his own thoughts, of his disappointment or approval. In truth, he did not know what he felt, did not know if he had a right to feel anything. He knew only that he loved this fierce, small sister of his.

"What would you have me do?" he asked.

"Take me across the river," Itala said. "I must see for myself what has become of him."

Much might be said of Draven's journey with this sister. But let us not dwell on it just now. You need know only that Draven and Itala again traversed Hanna's rapids and continued beyond the bare promontory crested with its twisted tree. They moored their craft and plunged into thick growth, scarcely knowing where they went, for neither had ever seen this side of the river.

But soon enough they began to discern signs of war. They came upon ravaged farms, and neither looked too closely at the forms lying festering in the fields.

Their going was slow, for Itala was quickly exhausted. They spent the night in one of the few standing shelters they could find, and Draven fed his sister from meager supplies and took nothing for himself. He wished he could have convinced her to let him go alone, but she would not have it. And how could he argue with her? He had never felt the desperation of love he saw now torturing her.

So together they pressed on, hoping that in the midst of the terror clutching Rannul, Itala's absence would not be noticed. Draven himself was already as good as dead and forgotten.

Kahorn village, so it was said, stood a day's march beyond the river's banks. One of Hanna's branching tributaries flowed past it, so Draven knew they must search for water. But in the end they simply followed the path of destruction wreaked by Gaher and his men.

Until at last they stood on the edge of the forest, gazing down into what once must have been a thriving village center. Many sod houses, very like those of Rannul, lined either side of the tributary's banks, and fields and pastures surrounded, extending out as far as the eye could see.

But all was now charred ruin. The sod house roofs were blackened, and equally black and cold were the doorways, testimony to the furnaces so recently contained therein. The fields swirled with the ashes of decimated crops, and no sign of life could be discerned anywhere save for the cries of carrion crows.

From where she stood, Itala could see savaged bones.

She stared long and silently at this evil landscape. She was so quiet that Draven feared she had fallen into a stupor. At last, however, she turned to her brother, and in a voice strained with exhaustion and despair, she said, "He is dead then."

Draven put his arms around her and held her close as she wept.

FALL OF
TEARS

AKILUN'S VOICE, SPEAKING the strange language of his people, filled the girl's head with images so clear she may have looked upon them herself even as he spoke. When that last image passed before her vision—when she saw the devastation of Kahorn—she believed she saw it just as Itala had long ago.

Just as Itala wept then, so the girl buried her face in her hands and let her tears fall.

Akilun, who had worked slowly and meticulously in time to his own voice, stopped and turned to her. He spoke her name and asked, "Why do you weep so?"

At first the girl could not answer. She was too overcome with Itala's emotions. But slowly her mind resettled, became her own once more. Her vision cleared, and she was able to look into the Kind One's face illuminated so gently in the lantern light. Then she sniffed and rubbed her nose with the back of her hand. "I—I feel so sad," she said, which was already obvious enough. So she tried again to put her feelings into clearer words. "I feel so sorry for Itala. For the poor prisoner. For Callix, who died."

Then Akilun's brow, which had been puckered in concern, smoothed as he smiled. "Dear child, do not weep! The story is not done. Prince Callix wasn't dead."

"He wasn't?" The girl sat up straight, her eyes shining with sudden hope.

"No indeed," Akilun assured her. He lifted his tools again and set back to work. "No, for it was but a few days later, after Draven had returned his sister to Rannul village, that Itala received a sign . . ."

ARMS OUTSTRETCHED

CCATA DIED, AND another member of Rannul fell ill—a child not even come to his tenth year. There was no reasoning behind who was taken. No one who had touched or tended to the previous victims became sick. Man, woman, and now child . . . all were prey to this strange malady, without preference or exception that anyone, even the oldest medicine woman, could explain.

A sense of doom pervaded all. The villagers went about their daily work, but none seemed capable of raising their heads to face each new day. Each new day could so easily be their last. Anyone at any moment could fall prey to this agonizing sickness.

Having delivered Itala safely back home, Draven continued his practice of staying out of sight. He hunted and left his offerings at the village borders. Sometimes they were accepted. Sometimes they were ignored only to be dragged off by wild beasts. Nevertheless, he always brought them.

And he wondered about those things he had heard and seen. No one else seemed to have discovered the finger-shaped bruises he had glimpsed on Oson's dead body, and he did not know to whom he could mention them. Were they merely bruises Oson had received in the heat of battle? Or did they, as Draven suspected, pertain to the unearthly manner of his death?

It hardly mattered either way. Nothing could be done, Draven knew. Nothing but continue to exist until one met with a brutal death. A coward's attitude, to be sure, but what was he if not a coward?

But Itala . . . her heart was differently set.

She found her brother while he was on the hunt, rooting him out of hiding with far more ease than pleased his pride. Her crashing through the underbrush drove away all game, and she called to him loudly every few steps. He almost tried to slip away, irritated at her for spoiling his hunt. Instead he rose up from hiding and stood with a spear gripped in his fist as she hobbled up to him.

In her hand, she clutched a wreath of red asters; asters, which were not yet in season, and therefore a strange sight to behold.

"Brother!" Itala cried, lifting the blossoms high like a banner. "Brother, I found these outside my door this morning."

"Indeed?" said Draven, frowning at her. Upon closer inspection he saw that the asters had been carefully dried to preserve their color and shape. "Did you prepare them for some—"

"No, no!" Itala cried. "I found them like this. Woven into a ring. Someone brought them." She stood before him breathing hard, leaning heavily on her crutch. "I believe Callix brought them," she said. "He knew. He knew about the asters that bloomed just before I slew

Hydrus. I told him, and he knew. This is a sign. He is alive. He is alive and near!"

The voices of the night were many and varied, and the Prince of Kahorn knew them all. He knew the humming chorus of crickets in the grass and little biters in the air. He knew the liquid, deep-throated boom of bitterns strutting in the marshy places along the river's bank. He knew the voice of the river herself—of Hanna, the sometimes gentle, sometimes vicious mother of this great land. Far off, he heard the lonely howl of wolves, an eerie harmony to the nearer sounds.

Callix knew the songs of evening, and he feared none of them. What he feared was the silence. The silence underlying everything now.

The silence flowing down from the empty crest of the promontory.

He felt it, though he did not look at it, the high bare peak where the twisted tree stood. He hated being so near to it but could not bring himself to leave. Not yet. He would give her until dawn. If she did not come, then he, broken by yet another loss, would take up his spear and go, pursuing the weary footsteps of his people already marching far away from this land that was once their home.

Home had been stripped from them—the raiding warriors of Rannul but the final stroke of the knife.

Another familiar sound struck Callix's ear: the dip and pull of a paddle on the water. He leaned out from hiding, gazing upriver. The moonlight showed a canoe approaching from the opposite shore. He knew it must be Itala. He also knew that she must have convinced her powerful brother to carry his canoe far downriver to a crossing point below the rapids. That, or they had taken the same harrowing, moonlit journey Callix and Draven had made a year ago. Somehow, Callix doubted Draven would put his sister at such risk.

The canoe trailed a diagonal path across the broad surface of Hanna, coming to rest not far from where Callix waited. Just as Callix had hoped, Draven remembered the place he had moored his craft when he helped his enemy escape and grounded it there again now.

Itala stumbled as she tried to climb from the canoe on her own, nearly falling flat on her face. Callix stepped forward, but Draven was much closer. He caught his sister, and she leaned heavily against him. Then she growled, "Leave me, I don't need help!"

Draven snorted but made no other protest. He took a step back, and both of them saw Callix approaching. Itala gasped, and Draven's hand went for a weapon. But the next moment, by some miracle of sight or second sight, Itala recognized the shadowy form.

"Callix!" she cried and staggered toward him, forgetting her crutch and stepping painfully with her clubfoot. He leapt forward and relieved her of the pain by catching her in his arms. Draven, embarrassed, turned away and gave them a private moment of desperate gladness.

"I was so afraid for you," Itala said, holding her beloved close.

"And I, for you," Callix replied. "Tell me, Itala, has the . . . have your people—"

"Yes." Itala growled the word, pulling back and glaring fiercely up into the destitute prince's face. "Yes, the curse of which you warned me has now attacked Rannul. And I am glad of it! After what we have done, I am glad of it."

Her angry voice emphasized her ugly words, but Callix shook his head. "No. Never be glad of such evil. I am only sorry it has spread, and I doubt now that it will ever stop." He put his face close to Itala's, his forehead pressed to hers. "My dear one, come away with me. The remnants of Kahorn are leaving this land, following the rising sun to see what new life it might illuminate for us. Perhaps if we go far enough we might escape both this bitter war and this far more bitter malady. But I cannot bear to go without you! You must come. Please."

Itala's skin was pale in the moonlight, and her eyes were like two enormous stars, filled with tears. "My love," she said, "what manner of coward would I be to leave my own people while they suffer so? We deserve our fate, but I cannot pretend that I am not a daughter of Rannul. I cannot forget my father and forefathers so easily."

Callix gazed earnestly into her eyes. He saw there that she did not speak the whole truth. Though her words were courageous, fear, deep fear scored lines in her face. The stranglehold of her heritage was mighty indeed. There was at least one man in this world whom Itala truly dreaded. She would not cross Gaher.

"I would never be able to forgive myself," she said. Her words did not lie, but neither did they speak the whole truth.

How he wanted to argue. To plead, even to rage. But he loved this proud young woman too dearly. So Callix saluted her with a kiss upon her forehead then stepped back and bowed low. "You are your own mistress, Itala. I honor your decision." Though it broke his heart to speak the words, there was no good in waiting, no good in straining this painful farewell to the breaking point. "I wish you long life and happiness. And I will never forget you."

"Callix!" She spoke his name too softly for him to hear as he retreated from sight. In a moment he was gone, swallowed up by the forest. Her sharp ears listened to his retreat until he had passed beyond hearing as well.

Itala wrapped her arms tightly around her weak body and cursed her weak spirit. Who was she to claim any courage for herself? She had slain Hydrus, to be sure, but that was such an easy task by comparison to this. In this venture, this crisis moment of her life, she knew she had failed.

But she would not risk the terror of running from her father.

Slowly she turned and tried to take a few steps toward her brother.

She stumbled and fell to her knees.

Draven covered the space between them and stooped to assist his sister. She clutched his arm, leaning her head against his fur-clad shoulder. "They're going away," she said, her voice even but straining to remain so. "They're traveling east, and they won't return."

Draven said nothing. After all, it was probably for the best of all concerned. He could see no future for Itala and her father's enemy. Another war party from Rannul would surely wipe out the last of Kahorn. No, it was for the best that they left, the prince and his people.

He helped his sister up and assisted her back into the canoe. Splashing in the shallows, he shoved the canoe off then climbed inside and took up his paddle. He stroked against the river's current, working to get them both as far upriver as possible before the rapids' flow became too strong.

At last they put to shore. Itala climbed out before he could help her, grabbed her crutch, and began pushing her way through the thick-grown foliage. He pulled his canoe high up onto the shore and left it before hastening after his sister. He walked behind her for a while, allowing her the privacy to weep or rage as she needed. He could not tell which way her heavy spirit tended, for she was silent.

There were no paths this far downriver from the village, and their going was slow in the darkness. He stepped forward at last and asked, "Will you rest?"

"No," she replied and kept on, though he knew she must be exhausted to the point of fainting. But Itala would punish her body, as though by so doing she could earn some penance for her heart. Her coward's heart that would not permit her to stand up to the wrath of Gaher.

At last she fell heavily against a tree and did not move save to breathe. Draven stood by and did not touch her. Very quietly, as though confessing a sin, she said, "I cannot go on."

"Never mind," Draven replied, and he picked her up. She was slight, and he broad and strong. Nevertheless, their going was slow, and Draven was obliged to choose his way carefully through the thick trees and undergrowth. He felt the eyes of the night upon them, but none belonged to any creature brave enough to accost him.

Just as dawn approached, they came to more familiar territory, close to the village. A keening wail went up with the rising sun, and both Draven and Itala knew that the child possessed of the convulsing sickness had died.

"Put me down, brother," Itala said then. "I will walk the rest of the way."

The stern pride in her voice was command enough. Draven obeyed, and they continued very slowly back to the village. The mourning of Rannul reached out to greet them as they stepped from the forest into one of the outlying fields.

Suddenly Itala stopped, her eyes narrowing. By the light of grey morning's approach, she saw a shadow flicker along the ground. She looked up to see what might have caused it. Some hawk or other raptor, perhaps. But no, there was nothing.

She returned her gaze to the ground, searching for that dark, insubstantial movement. Nothing at first and then . . . yes. There it was. A shadow without source, moving swiftly across the field. And it was coming straight for them.

Itala gasped. For she saw in that momentary glimpse that the shadow reached out two long arms, two long-fingered hands.

Before she could speak, the shade was upon them. Her brother fell down heavily at her side. He kicked her crutch with one flailing leg, and Itala plummeted to earth. She covered her face with her arms, for Draven's whole body convulsed so violently that he could have done her serious injury. She rolled away from him, screaming, "Gaho! Gaho!" in her terror.

For Draven was lost to himself, lost in a storm of pain. Foam fell from his lips, foam and blood as well, for he had bitten his tongue. He may have tried to struggle, but it was no use. Itala pushed herself upright, staring at the horror before her. She screamed his childhood name again and again, as though somehow she could make him hear her, as though somehow she could draw him out of his agony.

Then suddenly across her mind's eye she glimpsed again the shadow. The shadow with the reaching arms. And she knew, though she could not see it, that this shadow clutched her brother even now with those long fingers and shook him to his core.

Itala grabbed her crutch and used it to push herself upright. Then she dropped it and, ignoring the shooting fire up her leg, lunged at her flailing brother. Her hands grasped at what she could not see, could not feel, but what she knew was there.

She caught the monster and wrenched it harshly.

Draven gave one last great cry. Then he lay still, unfeeling, unseeing. His eyes stared at the sky above him, golden now with the sunrise, but his gaze was empty.

Then, just as the sun crested the far horizon, he blinked and came to himself. He felt the field grasses tickling his face. Clouds moved slowly across his vision, high in the sky above. His heart galloped in his breast, and he spat blood from his mouth.

Only then did his ears begin to work. And he heard his sister's grunting pain.

Draven sat up and whirled around. Itala writhed on the ground, every muscle straining, her jaw tight, her teeth clenched. She looked as though something beat her, worried her like a wolf savaging its prey. But there was nothing to be seen.

Then she was still. Just as Draven had witnessed with the others, the episode passed, leaving her gasping for air and unconscious.

"Ita!" he cried. The next moment she was in his arms and he was running for the village, shouting for help.

A HARD
TALE

THE GIRL WAS VERY quiet that night as she stared into the evening fire. Her family was busy and bustling all around her, her eldest sister boasting of her prowess at the hunt even as the results of her day's work roasted over the flames. Iulia scolded the littlest ones and called out orders to her big sons and her husband, all of whom obeyed her with mild good humor.

But the girl simply sat, her back against a boulder as a protection from the night surrounding. Her knees were drawn up to her chest, her arms wrapped tightly around them. She stared at the flames but did not see them.

Strange images formed by the Kind One's words filled her eyes.

He had stopped abruptly and turned to her just as the story reached its crisis moment. She could not believe that he would end the tale there, with Itala succumbed to the sickness! But he had gazed at her thoughtfully and said, "I'm sorry, Iulia's daughter, but I must stop now. It is getting late, and I have other tasks to which I must attend." He knelt before her, his eyes looking deep into hers. "I don't think I am the one best suited to tell the next part of this tale in any case."

And so he sent the girl on her way. Though the sun was still high, she had all but fled down the track, certain that invisible eyes watched her from the shadows of the forest surrounding. She'd reached her village panting, and her heart had scarcely calmed its frantic beating in the hours since.

She didn't want to eat. When food was passed her way, she nibbled only a few mouthfuls then sent it on. No one noticed, for she took care that they should not. But when she rose at last to enter her mother's hut and lie down for sleep, she saw her grandmother's eyes fixed upon her with a knowing gaze. She hoped Grandmother would not ask her about the story tomorrow. But she knew this was a futile hope.

The girl scarcely slept that night. She kept believing she saw long, shadowy arms reaching across the open doorway. She believed she heard voices upraised in agonized cries, and though she told herself these were nothing but night owls, she could not make her imagination believe.

The next morning she rose up exhausted to go about her daily tasks. She tried to slip away to one of the outer gardens, but her mother caught her with a word.

"Child!" Iulia said. "I need you to take your grandmother to the river now. Hurry along!"

The girl turned slowly and found her grandmother leaning heavily on the doorpost of her private hut. Iulia stood nearby, beckoning. There could be no argument.

The girl obeyed. She felt the weight of her grandmother's arm on her shoulder, and though she normally did not mind, she thought it a great burden on this morning. Their progress was slow, slower than usual even, and grandmother said next to nothing. The girl helped the old woman to wash her face and hands. Then Grandmother removed her leg wrappings and shoes and put her feet into Hanna's gentle shallows, her old face relaxing, though all the lines remained as clearly defined as ever. She closed her eyes, allowing the sun to warm her pale, thin skin. Then she spoke without looking at her granddaughter:

"Will you return to the Great House today?"

"No," the girl replied, too quickly. She wished she could take back her response; she wished she could turn it into a variety of excuses. But she knew the tone of her voice had been all too clear, and nothing would fool her grandmother.

Slowly the old woman lifted one foot from the water, grimacing. The air was cool that morning, the wind sharp as it darted along the river's surface. Grandmother opened her eyes and watched the water dripping from her foot then lowered it back down. She continued to not look at her granddaughter. "Are you afraid?"

There was no good in lying. Not to Grandmother.

"Yes," the girl said. "I'm afraid for . . . for Itala. I don't want to hear how she died."

Only then did Grandmother turn her face to the girl, her brow wrinkled with, perhaps, sorrow. "It is a hard tale, my child," she said. "But it is a good one. It is one you should hear to its end."

The girl shook her head. "I'm afraid," she said again.

"So was Draven."

At these words the girl's eyes kindled with interest she could not suppress. For though she feared to hear the end of this tale, her heart thudded in response to that name. Across her mind's eye flashed the face of Akilun's carving, and she saw, for the first time, just how much fear hid behind that stoic gaze. But then, he was the Coward. Of course he was afraid. Just like she was.

Grandmother put out her arms, and the girl entered her embrace, burying her head in the old woman's bony shoulder. She held on tight, as though clinging to a lifeline, even as her grandmother began to speak slowly, rhythmically, falling into the storyteller's cadence.

"Draven would not leave his sister's side," she said.

RUMOR OF
HOPE

I N THE CENTER of the sod house was a fire pit, the coals scraped
flat but still glowing red. A thin stream of smoke rose up through
the hole in the roof. Moonlight pooled down from above, its pure
white glow blending with the deep glimmer of the embers. All was still.

Then Itala began to groan.

Draven, sitting beside her in the darkness, reached out and caught
her shoulders, holding her flat so that she could not, in her flailing, do
herself an injury. She convulsed, her body demonstrating surprising
strength, and he was forced to press most of his own weight into her
shoulders as he attempted to hold her still. In her mouth he'd tied a stout
stick to keep her clamping jaws from cutting her tongue or the inside of
her cheek.

The sight of her so muzzled was enough to bring tears to his eyes. So he blessed the darkness that blinded him.

The spasm passed. Itala lay panting beneath him. Draven drew a ragged breath and did what he could to make her comfortable. He eased her clubfoot back under the rugs, and he ran his fingers through her hair, pulling it back from her face and smoothing it.

She was so weak. So much weaker in body than Oson had been. And how long had Oson survived? Only three days.

Light flashed behind Draven, and he turned to see a torch appear in the doorway, borne by his father's hand. Gaher stepped into the small, closed-in space, seeming to fill it with his great bulk. He did not look at Draven. He never did these days, since Draven took on his new name and disgrace. Gaher behaved as though his son were already dead, his remains carried away in Hanna's flowing arms.

But his eyes fixed upon the face of his suffering daughter. For a moment he wasn't a warrior—he was a father. Anyone looking at him then would have seen the man who had defied all the urging of the village elders and insisted that his crippled daughter be allowed to live. They would have heard again the pride in his voice when he declared her his wolf pup and urged her to grow, to prove the true strength of her heart to all.

He crossed the short space between the door and Itala's sleeping rugs. Draven drew back quickly, avoiding even the touch of his father's shadow. Gaher knelt beside his daughter, his rough, scarred fingers tracing the line of her cheek then touching the stick tied in her mouth. He grimaced, like a snarl, but did not remove the stick.

He bowed his head then and whispered, "My fierce one. My Itala."

When he rose, he turned his back on Draven, refusing still to look at him. But when he reached the door he paused. His growling voice reached back through the shadows to touch Draven's ear.

"It should have been you. I wish that it was."

He took the light with him when he left, but it scarcely mattered. The darkness surrounding Draven was so heavy that no mere torchlight could pierce it.

How long he stood unmoving at the wall, he could not say. But when Itala groaned and began once more to convulse, Draven found his limbs inspired. He leapt to her side and braced again, doing all within his power to ease her in this spell of agony. The pain was so great, he knew she could not suffer it much longer and survive.

When she lay immobile again, he covered her with her rugs, smoothed her hair, and wiped the foaming spittle from her cheeks. The red glow of the embers gleamed in his eyes, which narrowed suddenly. He bent and, lifting up her hair, looked at her neck.

It seemed to him that he saw dark marks, as though something even now gripped her by the throat.

He sat back, his heart thudding in his throat. But though he stared into the empty space above his sister, he could not make himself believe that he saw anything, no matter how he tried. He reached out with both hands, and any who might have observed him would have thought he had gone mad, so daft did he appear as he sought to take hold of thin air. For there was nothing to grasp.

And yet—though he wasn't certain if it was a memory or a memory of a nightmare—he seemed to recall the sensation of long, long fingers grasping his own throat.

"Itala." He whispered her name hoarsely, crouching down to place his mouth close to her ear. "Ita, my dear one, I am lost and I am afraid. If only I possessed your courage!" Then he pressed a kiss to her forehead. The act itself was enough to undo him, and he gasped, choking on the pressure of a sob in his throat. He caught her face between his hands and touched his cheek to her forehead. "My sister," he said, feeling the pain of her every breath. "I must leave you. But hear my voice—hear me, Ita! Remember our hunt. Remember how you fought the pain, how you won your victory. Remember, Ita! And hold on until I return for you."

With this, he released her and stood. Pulling his fur cloak tightly across his shoulders, he ducked out of the sod house into the dimness of Rannul Village. Few fires lit that blighted night, for most of the villagers hid in their homes, afraid to venture out, afraid that they or their loved ones might bring some foul luck down upon themselves and catch the evil malady that even now beset their chieftain's daughter.

So it was that no one saw Gaher's disgraced son descend the path to the river. He chose one of the warriors' canoes at random and pushed it out into the water. Then, taking up his paddle, he stroked against the current, making his way up river with all speed. When he was well out of sight of Rannul Village, he put to shore, dragging the canoe into hiding among the trees.

He remembered what his sister had told him only the night before: "*They're traveling east, and they won't return.*"

So he plunged into the forests, traveling sometimes by narrow trails, sometimes crashing through underbrush. Birds and beasts fled at his coming, and he made no effort to move silently or disguise his path. He simply raced with all speed against the night and on into coming dawn.

As he ran he told himself, *They will be many and burdened. They cannot have gone far. They cannot have gone far!*

It was a hopeless quest, and he knew it. But he would not allow his heart to acknowledge what his head kept trying to insist. Over and over again he saw Itala, her body wracked and tortured, her face so twisted with pain that she was scarcely recognizable. This image drove him on, faster and farther, until his lungs pleaded for air and his limbs pleaded for rest.

He would give them neither. *They cannot have gone far!* he lied to himself.

Then, just as the sun rose over the horizon, spilling light across the world, Draven beheld a wonder. At his feet, just where his footsteps fell, red asters bloomed. Though their season would not arrive for many months yet he saw them, bright as drops of blood, a crimson trail spreading from where he even now ran, on through the forests.

He did not stop to think or reason. His heart was already desperate; why not place his trust in the impossible? Perhaps the airy gods had not abandoned him. Perhaps they had sent him a sign. In the trees overhead he heard a wood thrush sing its first morning song, and he recalled hearing the same song when he and Itala hunted Hydrus.

So he followed the trail of crimson blossoms, followed the lilting song of the thrush. He had taken only a few paces when the trees gave way and he found himself on a rocky outcropping overlooking a wide valley. A trail of burdened travelers, their backs bowed with their belongings, wound their way across the valley, making for the rising sun. The displaced tribe of Kahorn.

"Callix!" Draven cupped his hands around his mouth, putting all his heart and soul into that one great bellow. The world was so wide, the air so thick, he felt he could never throw his voice far enough, but this did not stop him. "Callix!" he cried again and again, and sometimes, "Kahorn!" He flung himself over the edge of the outcropping, slipping and sliding his way down, pausing only momentarily to shout again, "Callix! Kahorn!"

At the very back of the line the Prince of Kahorn walked, his hand clasping a staff, his heart heavy in his breast. He could scarcely raise his face to see the rising sun, so deep was his sorrow. He kept thinking of Itala, recalling their final conversation and their parting. Somehow he had known she would not come away with him. But how could he have left her so quickly? Left her, knowing full well what evil preyed even now upon her people.

His steps slowed. Soon he was far behind the rest, as though some anchor had caught hold of him between the shoulder blades and refused to set him free. If he left, she would surely die. If he stayed . . .

Faintly he heard a voice he almost recognized crying out his name.

"Callix! Callix!"

Startled, the Prince of Kahorn looked back over his shoulder. The sun cast its long beam far, illuminating the distant but swiftly approaching figure of Draven. His enemy. His savior.

Callix stood in amazed silence. Then he realized. He realized the only reason Draven could possibly be pursuing him now. His heart froze in his breast, and his eyes darkened even as he stood bathed in morning light.

He dropped his staff and ran, covering the distance between him and Draven as swiftly as he could. Soon he was close enough to see the pale lines of Draven's face, and he knew his fears were true.

"Itala!" he cried, unable to say more.

Draven, his whole body heaving with the exertion of his night-long run, bent double, his hands on his knees. Even so, he managed to gasp out, "Yes. It took her."

Everything in Callix's spirit wanted to cry out. But he could neither speak nor move. He could only stand in numb horror, watching until Draven finally caught his breath. Then Draven straightened, towering above the Kahorn prince as he always had.

"Tell me," he demanded, "what happened to Kahorn."

"You know what happened," Callix replied, his voice dull with dread. "What you have seen taking place in Rannul . . . that is what happened in Kahorn. It had been happening for many months before you and I met. It continued the whole of spring, summer, winter . . . on until the following spring. When your people attacked, we were so weakened.

Weakened by many deaths, weakened still more by fear." He cursed then, bitterly, and his hands clenched into fists. "I warned you not to let your people cross the river," he said, his eyes flashing with rage, possibly with tears. "I warned you, Draven."

The next moment, a powerful grip lifted the prince by the front of his shirt almost off his feet. He found his face close to Draven's, and the expression in that young bear-of-a-man's eye was more terrifying than anything he had faced in the war with Rannul.

"What are you not telling me?" Draven growled. "What do you know that you are not saying?"

Callix was no coward, but his courage failed him for that moment. Then he caught at the arm arresting him and twisted it hard, just managing to escape Draven's grasp. He backed away quickly, for he thought Draven's fury such that he might slay him, even as he should have a year ago when claiming his man's name. Neither of them bore any weapon, so they circled each other like two wolves.

"Did all who suffered from this sickness die?" Draven demanded.

"Yes. All," Callix replied. "Not one who fell prey was spared."

"Then what are you not telling me?" Draven said again. "Why were you found alone so close to Rannul territory? What were you doing? What do you know about that promontory?"

And so the disgraced prince and the displaced prince faced off, each striving against the will of the other. But Callix saw in his enemy's face a love of Itala that reflected his own. A love that was possibly deeper still, for the roots of brother-and-sister bond grow from the same soil.

Callix stood down, placing his hand on his heart in a gesture of submission. Draven, seeing that gesture, relaxed his stance. "Tell me what you know," he said, his voice pleading as much as it commanded.

So Callix told him: "It is said among my people that the forest growing atop that certain promontory on the bank of Hanna is not a forest of our own world. Indeed, it grows in a place that exists on the edge of our very dreams. Kahorn has always revered that high place."

He shook his head then, for a shadow seemed to grip his soul as he remembered a not-too-distant past. "One day we looked up and saw that the wood on the crown of the promontory was gone. Vanished, as though hewn down in a single night. When we drew nearer, we saw instead a single tree, apparently dead, standing on the very crest. We knew it was a bad omen, for we saw a carrion bird circle as though to land, only to change course and fly far away, out of sight. We could not guess what the omen would mean.

"Only one day later the first of our people fell prey to the sickness you have now witnessed. And so it continued, day after day. As soon as one died, another would take ill. Only ever one at a time. Some would live on up to four days, even five. Some lasted not even a day. All succumbed, no matter our prayers, no matter our pleas to the airy gods."

Draven nodded. But he had not come all this way only to learn what he already knew: that the gods did not care for the fates of men. "What did you do?" he asked. For he suspected Callix was one who would search out answers even when no answers were to be found.

"As I told you," Callix continued, "my people have many stories about the forest on that hilltop. One such story claims that if a man enters that forest, stepping out of this world into the other, and calls out, 'Mercy!' then mercy will come to him." He shrugged, his fists opening in a helpless gesture. "What could I do? The forest growing up the hillside was still intact. I thought perhaps I might enter, might try to discover if the legend is true. I thought I might call for mercy in the Wood and see if mercy would come to me."

"Did you?"

"No. I set out with a small party, but we were caught by men of Rannul, who had entered our territory unknown to us. My companions were slain, and I was taken to your village. When you helped me escape, I was sick unto death. I could not risk the Wood in such a state. It took me many days to make my way home, and then I lay in fever for some while I do not recall. After that . . ." He bowed his head, ashamed of what he must say next. "After that, when I traveled again with the same purpose at heart, I chanced to see you and . . . and Itala. I saw her hunt the great fish. I saw how she, crippled though she was, faced that monster, willing to die for the sake of the mighty hunt. I knew that I could not step beyond my own world, perhaps never to find my way back again, without . . . without speaking to her first."

Draven studied the prince before him, his brow drawn into a stern line. He wondered if he despised Callix but thought perhaps not. After all, his sister was a young woman like no other. And he considered the many mad dreams he had entertained concerning fair Lenila, which he might well have enacted were he not such a coward. No, he could not blame the Kahorn prince for his choices.

"Is it true?" he asked. "What your people say? This tale of mercy and of other worlds?"

"I do not know," Callix admitted. "I know only what I have told you." Then he cried out, "Wait! Where are you going?"

Draven, already striding back the way he had just come, called over his shoulder, "I'm going to find out!"

"Then I will come with you," the Prince of Kahorn declared.

They said nothing, these two solemn princes, as they made their way back across the wild territory beyond Kahorn. Each intent upon his purpose, they understood one another well enough without words. Their journey was long, but they faced no foe along the way . . . no foe save for the passage of time.

For the sun, marking his course across the sky, seemed to warn them with each passing hour: *She will not last much longer. She cannot last much longer.*

So they traveled with all possible speed, sometimes Draven in the lead, sometimes Callix. At last they drew near territory well known to Callix, and he spoke for the first time since their conversation that dawn: "We are near."

Soon after, Draven heard the voice of the river and saw the peak of the promontory rising above the rest of the landscape, its bare crown open to the heavens. He saw the twisted tree at its summit, and the very sight made his stomach clench in knots. Once more he felt what a coward he was. But his footsteps never faltered.

They approached a place near the foot of the promontory where Callix stopped cold. By the look on his face, Draven knew they had come to the beginning of the strange wood. But though he searched for some sign, Draven could discern no variation in the air or landscape before them. It was merely more forest climbing up the promontory slope, exactly like the forest through which they had traveled.

He felt his heart sinking. If this was the fabled Wood, what hope could there be for the equally fabled mercy?

Nevertheless, they had come this far. Perhaps it would be worth the climb to inspect the evil tree above. Draven took a step.

Callix caught him by the arm. "Are—are you sure you want to do this?"

Draven frowned at his enemy, his sister's beloved. He saw the truth of frightened belief in that young man's face. Still he could not make himself believe. He said only, "Itala is waiting."

This was sufficient. Callix relaxed his hold. Together the two of them stepped into the Wood.

The moment he passed into the shadow of those trees, Draven knew he had been wrong to doubt. For, though no discernible change occurred, a sensation beyond anything he understood—a sensation rooted deep down in his heart—told him he had left his world behind. If he were to turn around and try to retrace his steps, he would never find his way back out again. His own world was gone.

Trees surrounded them, foliage so dense as to become a sort of shield. Not a sound could be heard, no animal's voice, no bird's song, nor even the babble of the river. But the trees themselves seemed to watch the two mortals in their midst, and the scrutiny of the trees was neither kind nor welcoming. A silent whisper passed from one to the next, and Draven felt that the trees were plotting against them, planning their demise—though where this thought came from he could not begin to guess.

Then suddenly Callix broke the silence. "Mercy!" he cried.

Draven, remembering what Callix had told him, took up the cry himself. "Mercy!" he said, in echo of his enemy.

The two of them, shoulder to shoulder, progressed further into the shadows, pushing their way through branches that seemed to clutch at them. "Mercy! Mercy! Mercy!" they shouted. The trees responded with menacing growls that could not be heard by the mortals' ears but reverberated in their guts.

"Mercy!" they cried, knowing their time grew short. On all sides, shadows loomed, deepening with each passing breath. Soon they would be overwhelmed in utter darkness, and then . . .

"Who calls upon the name of my Lord?"

The voice reached their ears like a promise, and both Draven and Callix turned to it with glad cries. "Mercy!" they shouted again and lunged through the last small gap in the shadows. For there a brilliant white light streamed through like a helping hand extended to a drowning man. They emerged from the thick-grown trees into a clearing filled with more of that same otherworldly light and stood blinking like newborn lambs, their hands upraised to shield their faces from the intensity of that glow.

"Again I charge you: Who are you who call upon the name of my Master?" the same voice asked, speaking from somewhere beyond the light.

"I am Draven the Coward," Draven responded at once, making gestures of supplication after the manner of Rannul. "I come on behalf of my sister who is courageous like no other, but who suffers under an evil sickness. Please, can you help her?"

The light dimmed, not in luminosity but in concentration, so that Draven and Callix both found their eyes able to discern the figure standing behind it. It was a man, and he held the light in a silver lantern. Or rather, the light seemed to rest there momentarily, although one had the sense, when looking at it, that it could not wholly be contained within such a simple frame.

The man himself was almost as wondrous as the light he bore. Tall and beautiful beyond the understanding of mortal man, his face glowing with the same light as he carried, and his eyes full of a deep, deep song.

"I am Akilun Ashiun, servant of the Lumil Eliasul," he said. "And I will help you and your sister if I can."

AN OLD, OLD STORY

"AKILUN?" THE GIRL GASPED, so startled at this turn of the story that she drew back from her grandmother's embrace and stared at the old woman. "Akilun? The Kind One?"

"The same," her grandmother replied.

"But . . . but . . ." The girl shook her head, struggling to make this new knowledge fit within her sphere of understanding. "But I thought this was an old story!"

"It is," her grandmother said. "An old, old story indeed. But Akilun is older still."

This was impossible. The girl was of an age at which anyone significantly taller seemed old, but even so she could not picture Akilun and his beautiful, youthful face as part of this tale. That would make him older than Grandmother, and how could that possibly be?

But it was even less possible to look into her grandmother's eyes and believe she told anything but the truth. And after all, had not Akilun himself told her that he knew Draven? Indeed, now that she thought about it, she remembered the Kind One speaking to her at their first meeting as she stood and looked upon his carving:

"He was a man I knew. Long ago by the years as counted in your world. But it seems only yesterday to me."

"Akilun is not of our kind, sweet child," her grandmother said, reaching out and smoothing the girl's hair behind her ear. "He is much older, much fairer, much wiser than we. But he comes to us now to bless us for a little while. Then he will move on. Sooner or later he and his brother will go."

Grandmother's words sank like stones into the girl's young heart. Though she was young, she loved with great passion, and she hated the idea of her life without the Kind One hard at work high upon the hill. But she knew, as her grandmother spoke, that the Brothers' work was almost complete. Sooner. It was sooner that he would leave, not later.

She bowed her head, wishing she could hide the tears that welled up in her eyes. Grandmother was much too quick, however, and spotted them with ease. Her tired hands took hold of the girl's shoulders and held her firmly. "This is why," she said, "you must climb the hill again today. You must learn the rest of the story as Akilun tells it. You must hear it to its end and treasure it up in your heart, the joy and the sorrow of it. You must have courage to hear such a tale and know it for what it is. To take hold of the truth of it. For if you don't, you will always wish you had. All your life you will wish it."

She caught the girl by the chin and forced her to look up. "My darling," she said, "will you go?"

"I will go, Grandmother," the girl replied.

The Strong One was in the yard when the girl reached the top of the promontory. He was carrying a massive load of stone on his shoulders. Peering out from the forest shadows, the girl saw that each stone was precisely carved in fluted grooves to fit smoothly one to the other. There were five on his back, and each one must have been heavy enough to crush the girl flat were it to fall upon her.

She shuddered at the sight. Such strength was more than she understood, and she thought the Strong One ferocious and beautiful.

To her horror he turned his head and caught sight of her where she lingered in the shadows of the trees. He paused and shrugged the great weight from his shoulders, taking a moment to stretch his back. "Have you come with the water gift?" he asked, and she could tell that he was trying very hard to make his voice welcoming.

It didn't matter. She was still afraid. And she realized, to her horror, that she had not even considered the water gift when, after seeing Grandmother settled back in the village, she took to her heels and raced with all speed up the promontory path. What a fool she was to forget the one small thing the Brothers asked of Kallias Village!

The Strong One must have seen and interpreted the consternation in her face. "Never mind, little one," he said, offering a smile that was all the more terrible for its beauty. "It is of no concern. Are you come to see my brother?"

She nodded, pressing herself against the trunk of a tree as though it were a mother willing to hold her close.

"Well," said the Strong One, "he is hard at work at the moment. We are close to completion, you see, very close indeed."

And so he would dismiss her. So he would send her back down the path, never to hear the end of Draven's tale. But she couldn't bear it! She couldn't go back now, the tale untold, the truth unlearned.

The Strong One bent to pick up his load again, saying as he did so, "Run along, child. Akilun will see you tomorrow or the next day perhaps."

The girl couldn't find a voice with which to protest. But in her head she heard her spirit shouting *No! No, I can't go away! People are always telling me to run along. But I can't. Not now. I must know—I must know what happened! It's . . . it's . . .*

It's important.

To the falling of the sun.

To the rising of the moon.

To the turning of each day into each year.

To the drawing of breath, to every single beat of her heart from this moment on to her very last.

It was important that she learn the truth of this story. For though it happened long ago, in a deep and vital way it was still happening now and would go on happening forever. And if she did not learn it and grasp hold of it tightly with both hands, it would go on without her . . . still vital, still true. But she herself would be less true.

All these thoughts were confused in her head, like the inexplicable Faerie language in which Akilun spoke. She could never have put into words the tremendous tumult of ideas and fears crashing around within the narrow confines of her skull. She would strive all her life to learn the mortal words needed to express what she felt, and even then only if she heard the story today. Here at the dawning of her awareness, that tender threshold between childhood and adulthood when all is new and all is old simultaneously. That thin slice of time when mortality understands immortality without effort, with unconscious trust.

Still the girl stood frozen, leaning against the tree and staring at the strange, otherworldly man. He met her gaze, and though his expression was at first the patient sort that grown people wear when dealing with young, foolish children, slowly a change came across it. Almost . . . *almost* he seemed to grasp all those things the girl could not say with mere words but wished so desperately to communicate.

"Etanun, why do you stand there like a dumb kobold? Were you not urging for greater efficiency but an hour ago?"

The girl startled at the sound of Akilun's approaching voice, but the Strong One continued looking at her for a long moment more and did not turn to his brother until Akilun stood beside him. By then Akilun had seen the cause of his brother's delay. "Ah!" he said, smiling warmly in welcome. "So you've come back after all. I had feared you would not return."

"I—I—" The girl wanted to explain but still could put no voice to her many fears and many longings.

The Strong One, not perceiving her stutters, spoke in a low rumble perhaps not intended to be overheard: "We don't have time to delay. We are so close to completion."

Akilun replied in a voice like his brother's and yet very different, "We do have time. Remember, this is why we came into this world."

"I thought we came to build a House," Etanun said, his voice sharp.

"We did," said his brother. "And to that end we labor. But the House we build is to hold the light of Asha, and it must outlast all structures of brick and mortar."

Etanun looked as though he wanted to protest. Indeed, he opened his mouth as though to continue his arguments. But instead he glanced at the girl crouched in the shadows. Perhaps he saw just how deep those shadows were and how much deeper they might become in time.

So he said nothing but "Very well" and sighed deeply, as though he had just conceded a battle. Without another word, he lifted and carried his burden on around to a far wing of the House, out of sight. Soon the air rang with the song of his hammer on stone.

Akilun put out his hand. "Would you like to see Draven?" he asked the girl.

She nodded and, stepping into the stone-paved yard, slipped her small hand into Akilun's great one. They crossed the distance to the carved doors together. While holding Akilun's hand, the girl felt that her vision was made stronger. The fantastical carvings on the doors did not change shape, altering into images she recognized, but remained fantastical—hind-footed women, winged horses, eagle-headed lions. All images she could not comprehend, but she no longer felt she needed to. She could look upon them and accept them without comprehension. Just so long as she held onto Akilun's hand.

"Did your grandmother tell you more of the story?" Akilun asked as he pushed the heavy door, allowing a sliver of space for the two of them to pass into the cool darkness of the great hall.

"Yes," the girl said. As she followed his lead through the cavernous space, she told him of Draven's hunt for the Kahorn prince and their subsequent travels into the strange Wood outside their world. "And there they met *you*!" she finished, her soft voice scarcely more than a whisper but full of enthusiasm.

"Indeed they did," said Akilun, and guided her the last few paces into the circle of his silver lantern's light. The girl gazed up at the carving of Draven. She drew in her breath, amazed.

It was almost complete. Only his hand and whatever he held there remained unformed. The rest she saw with total clarity, down to the very fibers of fur lining each of his boots. Now she could see that he was descending some stairway, one foot lowered, not quite reaching the last step. This was why his gaze always seemed to her to be down-turned, his eyes meeting hers. He wasn't looking at her after all. He was watching his step.

The girl blinked. When her eyes opened again, she felt her breath stop horribly in her throat. For an instant the image of Draven was gone. In its place she saw again the twisted arms of a great dead tree. Or rather, not a dead tree—a tree that went on living though the true life of it was gutted out, leaving only the shell of ongoing existence. It was like the husk of an old man who had never proven his courage; the withered frame of an old woman who had never given her love.

The girl took a backward step, but Akilun's hand holding hers would not allow her to step beyond the ring of lantern light. With another blink, the tree vanished and she saw again the carving of Draven boldly descending into whatever fate awaited him.

She turned her gaze up to Akilun. Though her face was round and immature, her eyes brimmed with a need for understanding. "What happened to him?" she asked. "Where is he going? What does he hold in his hand."

"Sit a while, and I will tell you," Akilun said. He let go of her then, allowing her to settle down before the statue. He took up his hammer and chisel and set about the final shaping as he spoke.

"I listened long as Draven and Callix poured out their story together, very much the same story I have been telling you. At last their words ran out, and though they asked me no questions, their eyes were full of hope and dread—equal in balance but ready to tilt."

THE
CANDLE

STANDING IN THE LIGHT of that magnificent lantern, Draven and Callix found it easier to speak of the recent events of their lives. It wasn't as though the darkness was made any less—indeed the shadows outside seemed much darker in contrast. But those same shadows suddenly didn't seem to *matter* as much. All evil appeared small and futile while one rested in that brilliant circle of light.

So the two mortals finished their joint tale and stood silent before the beautiful immortal. Draven wondered if perhaps he stood in the presence of one of the airy gods made manifest . . . but he dismissed this thought almost at once. This man, this Akilun Ashiun, was no god; he was much greater than the many invisible beings Draven both venerated and despised. Akilun was not a being to worship. And yet he was wonderful beyond description and carried distant worlds in the depths of his eyes.

But those eyes were solemn now as Akilun considered the tale presented to him along with the pleas for mercy.

"I believe I know this evil of which you tell," he said at last. "One of the Faerie-folk has broken across the boundaries into your world. His name is Yukka, and he is a devil the likes of which I have long prayed would never touch mortal kind."

Here Akilun broke off his speech, turning his gaze to the light held within his lantern, as though drinking in some strength he lacked. Only then did he continue: "Yukka and his brother, Guta, are beaters, or so they are called among the fey. They feed upon pain and will inflict a great deal as they feast. They have successfully sustained themselves for generations of your time on a single immortal life. But mortals cannot endure so much for so long. A single beater of Yukka's greed can destroy whole nations if he is not stopped."

Draven, with Callix standing silently beside him, listened to these strange words and felt his coward's heart sinking in his breast. He had seen the marks on Oson's throat and similar marks on Itala's. He did not doubt Akilun's words. Perhaps there was some comfort in this revelation, no matter how horrifying.

Callix, his voice thick in his throat, asked, "Can you stop him? This Yukka, this beater . . . can you kill him?"

At this, Akilun met Callix's gaze and nodded. But his face was very solemn. "I can, and I will if you ask me to."

"Then come at once!" Callix cried.

But Draven, reading more of the truth in Akilun's eyes interrupted with a sharp, "No. No, tell me first what you are not saying. Tell me what you fear to say."

Akilun bowed his head. "The moment I step into your world, Yukka will know. The light I carry is powerful, and he will sense it. And he will kill his current victim at once, swallowing down the last of her pain to make himself strong before he faces me."

Draven and Callix said nothing. Both thought of Itala lying so helpless in her agony, clutched in Yukka's invisible fingers.

"I can kill the beater," Akilun said. "But it will cost Itala's life."

The light of the lantern no longer mattered. The shadows all around loomed enormous once more, and the two mortals felt themselves powerless against them. When at last Callix could find his voice and speak, he said only, "Then there is no hope."

"Indeed that is not so!" Akilun was quick to reply. "There is always hope. But this hope is a dangerous one, and it requires a man of rare courage to face it.

"Here is your choice, mortals. You may invite me to your world, knowing full well that Itala will die but that I will conquer your foe, thus sparing both of your tribes and offering them a future. Or . . ."

Here, as his voice trailed off, Akilun plunged his hand into a pouch at his side and withdrew a candle. Neither Callix nor Draven knew what it was, for candles were unknown among their people. But they watched as Akilun held the wick into the depths of his white-gleaming lantern. A bright flare nearly blinded them, and both men raised their hands to shield their eyes. When they could bear to look again, Akilun held out the candle, which was quite tall and thin. Wax melted and ran down its sides, and from the wick bloomed a white flame.

"I offer you the light of Asha, which is taken from the hearth fires of the Moon herself," Akilun said. "It is not so powerful as the lantern's glow, but it is equally true.

"One of you must bear this light down into Yukka's pit. You will find this pit by its marker: a single, leafless tree, not dead yet like unto one that is dead, standing in a lonely place. The pit will descend in a spiral stair around its roots, and he who carries this light must pass all the way to the end of that stair. There he will see many grotesque sights, but these he must not gaze upon too long. Instead he must look for the roots of the tree . . . and to them hold this light so that they catch ablaze!

"Yukka will be taken by surprise. He will have no time to think or to prepare. He will want to kill the girl but must focus all his strength on protecting the roots of that tree. He cannot pause to kill Itala, not if he wants to survive.

"But he must not survive. You must make certain that he remains in the pit even as the tree burns and all collapses around him. He must be buried and dead or he will return to hunt again. Only take care!" Here Akilun's voice became imperative. "Take care that you, whichever of you ventures down, are not caught in Yukka's grasp. For he is not bound by the laws of mortals, and he can cross great distances in the blink of an eye. You must make certain he is buried, and you must make equally certain that you are not caught in the trap meant for him. As soon as you have seen him, flee. Do you understand? Flee, or you will die in the pit along with Yukka."

Akilun stood in silence then, holding out the candle. The choice he offered lingered in the air between him and the two mortals.

Then Callix made a forward step and took the candle in his hands. The running wax dripped on his gloves, and he grimaced but did not allow the light to drop. "We will slay this beast," he said. "We will save Itala."

Akilun nodded. Then he turned where he stood and shined the beam of his lantern into the forest. A path opened up through the trees and the shadows, straight and true. At the end of it, Draven and Callix saw open ground.

"That is your way, the passage back into your world," Akilun said. "Follow it swiftly. I will wait and listen to the wind until I hear word of

Yukka's demise. Then I shall enter your world myself and see what I can do to repair the damage left in the beater's wake."

He clasped both men by the hand in farewell. But though Callix proceeded first, carrying the candle, it was Draven whose hand Akilun held onto longer than necessary and to whom he whispered with perilous urgency: "May Lumé light your way and Hymlumé bless your steps. And may you hear the Spheres singing your true name in the darkest reaches of your world."

Draven gazed into the worlds held in Akilun's eyes and believed he saw the very Spheres of which Akilun spoke.

But he knew his true name. Had not his father declared it already at the dawning of his manhood? He let go of Akilun's hand and followed swiftly behind Callix.

The liberation of stepping out of the strange Wood and back into their own world was enough to leave both young men gasping. But their relief was short-lived, for the moment they caught their breath, they found that they stood upon a bare incline. The voice of River Hanna rose up from below, filling their ears. Both knew exactly where they were.

Ahead of them, a goodly distance away at the top of the promontory, the bare branches of the twisted tree clawed at the sky.

Callix, clutching the candle with one hand and supporting that hand with his other, turned a sickened gaze upon Draven. "We are on the hillside," he said. "We are near."

Draven, however, looked out across Hanna to the territory on the far shore. The sun was setting heavily now, and he wondered if it were the same day. For they had stepped outside of their world, outside of their time. Could not many days have passed in what felt like mere minutes?

Could Itala even now be dead and laid out in her funeral canoe?

He saw the curling smoke of Rannul's fire pits, and his heart reached across the distance to that darkened sod house where he had last seen his sister. He knew—somehow he *knew* that she must still be alive. Even if only just.

He turned to Callix then. "Give me the light," he said.

Callix did not obey, only tightening his hold on the candle. "There is no reason for both of us to descend into this pit. Akilun said only one was needed."

"You are right," said Draven.

In that instant he flew at the Kahorn prince and wrapped his great arms tightly around him. Callix gave a cry, but he was pinned in Draven's hold. He dropped the candle in his efforts to twist free, and for a heart-wrenching moment he feared the light would go out. It did not, however, but lay burning upon the dirt even as Draven and Callix fell, striving against each other. More than a year had passed since their last fight and, despite his outcast cowardice, Draven had only grown stronger, while Callix's shoulder had never fully healed from the wound inflicted by Gaher's ax. He felt the weakness of it as he tried to fend off Draven's blows.

It was no use. Draven struck him across the head, and Callix fell unconscious beneath that blow.

Draven sat back, breathing heavily. For a fearful moment he wondered if he had slain his sister's beloved. But a quick check for a heartbeat told him that Callix lived. Indeed, he might not remain unconscious for long but could wake shortly.

Draven grasped the prince under the arms from behind and dragged him back among the trees. There he propped him against a trunk, removed his own belt, and bound Callix with it as tightly as he could. Then, wiping sweat from his brow, he turned and hastened back up the incline. He caught up the candle in passing and felt the life of its flame pulsing through the wax, down into the palm of his hand.

Alone he approached Yukka's twisted tree.

SPIRAL INTO DARKNESS

THE TREE ROSE ABOVE the center of the pit, its long roots clutching the stony ground. A steep descent spiraled around it into darkness so deep no mortal eye could discern the bottom. It might easily cut through the rock of the hill all the way down to the river far below.

As Draven approached the tree and the pit, his hand clutching the candle shook. He muttered curses upon his cowardice with each faltering step, but no curse could give him courage. Nevertheless, sore afraid, he drew near to the tree. He felt as though it laughed at him mockingly in the language of trees.

A foul stench rose from the pit; the stench of agony made sweet. Draven's stomach churned, and he doubled over, heaving. But he had not eaten in so long that his stomach held nothing to give up. Even so, some moments passed before he could draw himself upright and, holding the candle out before him, kneel on the pit's edge.

But there was no use in trying to see what waited below. He would have to descend.

Out of habit rather than belief, he breathed prayers to the airy gods. Then he took a first step down the incline, afraid that his foot would slip, for to all appearances the way down was slick and smooth, offering nothing for a man to rest his weight upon. To his surprise, however, he felt something solidify under his foot. So his vision changed even as the light of the candle reached out before him. The smooth rock became a jagged but sturdy stairway.

He continued his descent, casting his shadow behind him. He felt the pale ghost of a life in the tree roots reaching down into the rock on one side, and utter death in the soil on his other side. He had not realized until now how much life could be found in dirt and stone . . . not until it was sucked away, leaving behind that which surrounded him.

Soon the light of the opening above was a pinprick. He felt darkness closing in overhead, pressing close on the edges of the candle light. And what a small, frail light it was! Nothing like the glorious lantern. Oh, if only he had been given *that* light to carry then maybe he would not fear. But this one was so little.

Little like Itala. His fierce sister. She never let her size define the boundaries of her courage.

She had known, Draven thought. She had known what the monster was. The further he descended into the pit, the more certain he became. He recalled the clutching fingers on his own throat and knew that it should be he lying prostrate in pain, not his sister. But she had known. She had seen it, perhaps. And she had attacked it—brave, foolish, reckless girl! She had attacked the invisible monster and taken its curse upon herself to spare him.

"I won't let this beast be the end of you," Draven whispered. The closeness of the rock and roots around him made his voice seem small. But he growled the words even so. "I will set you free!"

He thought perhaps he must soon reach the level of the river and wondered if he would find himself up to his neck in water. But the next moment, all thought of the river vanished from his mind, for he stepped out of his world entirely. At the same moment, the light from the sky far above vanished.

Draven looked up the way he had come but could see no glimpse of the world he had left behind. The darkness of the pit was all around him, and it was the darkness of another world. A world where Faerie beasts lived and breathed and hunted. A world fit for the likes of Yukka and his evil hungers.

The sweet stench of pain was much stronger now. Even the flickering candle appeared affected by it, for its white light took on a greenish hue. A wild thought entered his head: Without the light, there would be no shadows. For shadows cannot exist without light. If the light went out . . . so must the shadows. There would remain only emptiness, and emptiness could not be so frightening.

It was so clear, such a perfect thought. Draven, standing on those rough stones far from air and sky, stared at the candle in his hand and felt the urge to put it out. To grind it into the stone wall beside him. To kill the light and thus kill the shadows. Surely then he would be safe.

He could not move, so strongly did the thought take him. He could only stand immobile and stare at the flame while darkness clawed in on all sides.

But as he stared he thought he glimpsed something. The white fire he held became, however briefly, the brilliant glow of the moon on a warm summer's night . . . the moon in the depths of winter . . . the moon on the verge of autumn or at the first birthing of spring. He saw the promise of change and the promise of sameness joined in one magnificent orb suspended in the night sky, ever shining.

A bit of the candlelight caught in his eye and embedded itself there, gleaming bright. And so he could raise his gaze and look on to the next step and the one after that. He could continue his descent, though his heart continued to quail in his breast. The candle lit his way.

It was then that the visions of which Akilun had warned him began.

Let us not speak too closely of those things Draven saw. Let it be known only that they were indeed ghastly, gruesome, presented in the full gore-laden glory in which such beasts as Yukka delight. Draven saw the pain of children—the flight, the capture, the brutal end. He saw these visions vividly, as though they happened even now, as though they continued happening over and over without end.

He knew then that he must have reached the bottom of the pit. For only in deepest depths could such things exist. A full garden of pain from which rose that sickly aroma. A mortal man would not have been able to bear it, would not have survived more than a few moments of those appalling sights.

But the candlelight was bright in Draven's eye now. Though he trembled with every step he took, he did not fall. He raised his candle high, searching for the exposed roots of the tree which must somewhere emerge from the stone into this cavernous space.

"It's too dark," Draven muttered. Raising his voice, he said, "I need more *light*."

Even as he spoke, both the candle and the gleam in his eye brightened, illuminating more of the space around him. The dreadful visions retreated to the very edge of his sight, and he clearly saw all the twists and turns of the caves here at the bottom of Yukka's pit.

He saw the tree roots, spread out much further than he had imagined.

Indeed, the tree itself in the mortal world up above was not half so big as any one of the enormous root extensions plunging from the cave ceiling into the ground. They were like the towering pillar trunks of the oldest, straightest trees in the forest. Small tendrils curled around them, natural-growing yet forming shapes and patterns too weird, too hideous to study closely.

These, then, Draven must set ablaze.

While the peril of Itala's position pressed heavily upon his mind, urging him to hasten about his task, Draven stood still, surveying the great roots. These spread apart from one another, each one a good six meters from the next. There were seven in all, and he would have to run the distance between them to set them on fire . . . and then somehow sprint to the spiral stair and climb back up before all this gave way.

He looked over his shoulder. Though he had taken only two, maybe three steps into the cavern, the stairway seemed much farther away than it should. The idea of putting more distance between himself and his only escape route made Draven's heart quiver with dread. Perhaps he could set fire to only one of the roots and it would be enough.

But that was a lie. A lie brought on by the sickening perfume all around him. A lie brought on by his coward's nature. He would never concede to such an impulse.

So he strode to the farthest root and stood before it. Though the tree up above had appeared all but dead, this root throbbed with sucking life. All the twists of its tendrils pulsated like veins. It did not look like any tree or root Draven had ever before seen. It looked animal. No, not animal. Far too unnatural for that.

Whatever it was—root, pincer, blood-sucking mouth—he knew that it was fixed not upon the stone to which it clung, but upon Itala herself. This root was as much a part of the invisible Yukka as those grasping hands of his.

Draven held up the candle. He touched it to the twining coils of wood and flesh made one. But the root was so big and the candle so small! How could a blaze possibly catch?

Leaning in, Draven blew gently on the flame so that it grew. He blew and he breathed a command that was almost a prayer: "Light it up, little flame! Light up this darkness!"

Suddenly the fire caught. With a blast that flung Draven from his feet, the root went up like a torch, flaming from floor to ceiling.

And in the sod house . . .

In the darkness . . .

Crouching on the mortal girl's chest . . .

Yukka sat up. His nostrils flared. His eyes gleamed. His hands tightened their chokehold.

He uttered one long, otherworldly scream that sent every man, woman, and child of Rannul falling to their knees. Then in a clap of thunder, he was gone.

Itala lay alone in the house, her face pale as death.

Draven scrambled to his feet, his arm upraised to shield his face from the tremendous heat of that fire. Smoke swiftly filled the caverns, making the walls seem much closer, much smaller than before.

Coughing, desperate to clear his lungs, Draven flung himself at the next root. He set the candle to it, and it caught fire much more quickly than the first. The blast of it knocked him back again, and he felt his skin blistering. The pain was immense, and the stench of his pain blended with the other perfumes in that poisonous air. But again he got up and again he continued to the next root, and the next.

Soon only one remained untouched. It glowed an angry red and white in the firelight, and the heat reflecting from its surface was so great that Draven could hardly bear to approach it. He felt the skin burning away from his hand as he extended the little white candle.

Just before the tiny flame touched the twisted root-skin something appeared behind Draven. Something with long fingers caught him by the shoulders. His ears filled with a shrieking unlike any voice he had ever before heard. Claws pierced through his thick fur cloak, down into his skin, and he screamed. He felt a rush of renewed power behind him as his pain fed into the beast on his back.

Grinding his teeth, Draven forced his body to take another step. One more, that's all he needed! At last the candle flame touched the final root, and half of Draven's hair burned away as the whole thing went up in roaring fire.

The beast on his back let go as Draven fell to the ground. He twisted in place and thought he saw a shadow flicking in and out among the pillars of fire. Draven's body spasmed with coughing, and he believed he must lie down and die, for he could not bear to move again, and the smoke was so thick, and his skin was blistered and blackened with burns.

But the candle's light was still in his eye. By that light, he saw the shadow of Yukka leaping for the stairway.

Sudden strength surged through Draven's soul, lending life to his failing body. He was on his feet and staggering between the flaming pillars, through the blackened smoke. With each step he found more strength offering itself to his limbs, and he took it and proceeded faster. He gained the stairway in a leap and, just as the first of the pillars fell and the cavern crumbled in after it, he sprang up that winding ascent. Another pillar broke, and ash and dirt nearly overwhelmed him. But Draven kept running, the candle held out before him. He made a turn and saw Yukka, or the shadow of Yukka. He saw the long-fingered hands grasping the stone walls on either side. The creature's strength was almost gone.

Overhead the sky gleamed. The world of mortals waited. What had Akilun said so short a while ago?

"*He must be buried and dead or he will return to hunt again.*"

The stairway was collapsing now, only a few paces behind Draven. He ran with all the strength left to him, his heart roaring with terror, his eyes bright with the candlelight. Itala had caught the beast. She had caught the shadow and held on fast. Which meant it *could be done.*

Draven leapt.

His empty hand—the one not holding the candle—latched onto Yukka's ankle.

The beast turned. Draven beheld red-flaming eyes. He felt the beater's hands pummeling his face, his arms, his chest. He did not let go. Even as he fell, and the crumbling walls closed in on top of him and the candlelight vanished and his eyes were blinded, even then he did not let go.

He fell with Yukka, and the collapsing cavern buried them both.

Still.

Still the candle's glow was caught in the coward's eyes.

Once caught, it cannot go out.

So he glimpsed the heavens. The Moon's great starry host of children. And he heard them singing. Singing to him as he died.

True Brother . . . Greater Love . . . Brave Heart . . .

He knew they sang his name.

THE FALLEN TREE

ITALA WOKE.

At first her body felt so numb that she did not know whether she were truly awake or merely lying in a semi-conscious paralysis, a lucid dream. Her clubfoot began to smart with pain that slowly ran up her leg, into her gut, and on up through her neck to fix in her brain. She lay, eyes closed, feeling the pain and along with it the return of her conscious self.

She realized suddenly that nothing clutched her neck.

Itala sat upright, gagging, her long hair falling about her face. She felt her neck, felt her face, felt all the bruises inflicted upon her. Her breath caught in her throat until she feared she would suffocate. But at last her body shuddered, her chest heaved, her lungs expanded. With a sob she fell forward, sucking air in and blowing it out.

Her teeth were clenched down upon a stick which was tied to her head. At first this realization made her angry. Who would bind her so ignobly? But then she recalled the wild convulsing of Oson and the others. Of Draven. If her strange, dark memories were true—if the beater had been pulverizing her body so that every limb flailed and every muscle strained—then whoever placed that stick in her mouth may very well have saved her from biting off her own tongue.

Fingers trembling, she worked to untie the cords, struggling, for the knots were fast. Who would have done this for her?

"Gaho," she said the moment the stick fell from her mouth into her lap. It must have been he. No other would take such care of her. No other would dare. She looked around her dark chamber. Night had fallen, yet no fire burned in the coal-heaped pit, no moon shone through the smoke hole. "Gaho?" she asked, this time questioning the shadows to see if her brother would answer.

But no answer came.

Itala put her hands to her neck and felt where the beater had held her so tight. She had known, in those brief moments of awareness before the pain overwhelmed her completely, that the creature—the devil— would never let her go. She was doomed like Oson, like Accata, like all the others.

Yet here she sat. Alone in the darkness. Truly alone, with no invisible devil to keep her company.

Suddenly she knew what must have taken place. How she knew, she could not say. But as she sat there searching the shadows, she also searched her heart. In her heart there was an empty place. Something was lost. And she knew what it was.

"Gaho!" she cried. Those outside her hut startled at the sound of her voice. Even Gaher, brave chieftain though he was, feared that he heard the voice of his daughter's ghost crying out in the darkness. But then they heard the scrape of Itala's crutch upon the ground, and Itala herself stuck her head out through the doorway. She was no ghost. They saw by the light of their torches that she lived.

"Daughter!" cried Gaher. "It is a miracle! An act of the gods!"

He stepped forward to take her in a huge embrace. But Itala startled back from him, her eyes wide, without recognition. The torchlight lit her face in harsh lines, and she looked feral and dangerous even to her mighty father.

"Gaho!" she cried again. "Where is Gaho?"

Her father said nothing, and the men beside him drew back, intimidated by the passion of her voice. No one could answer her, and none dared try. She stood in their midst, staring from one face to the next, finding no help in any of their gazes.

But a song reached across the great distance of the sky, a silver song that promised morning even in the deepest night. Itala heard it and turned toward the sound, turned toward the river. It was the thrush. The same morning thrush who had sung at dusk the day she hunted Hydrus.

The men of Rannul stood close all around. With a snarl, Itala shouldered her way between them. Hands reaching out in restraint were shrugged off, and once she even snapped her teeth like an angry cur. She almost fell, so great was her need for haste and so weak her limbs from the beating they had received. But she pushed on, leaning her full weight upon her clubfoot and ignoring the pain. After what she had experienced these last evil days, the pain of her twisted foot seemed as nothing.

The village of Rannul gathered, crying out in both delight and dread at the sight of their chieftain's daughter making her way through the village center and on down the path to the river. Some believed that in the wake of the horrible scream they had heard a few hours earlier, some greater evil must have struck. Perhaps the sickness now possessed Itala's limbs and was made mobile. Some men drew weapons, prepared to hack the girl down. Gaher leapt at these, barking commands they dared not disobey.

So all of them watched as the girl progressed at her painfully hobbled pace down to the water. She heard the song of the morning thrush again, across the water. It called to her, she knew.

Casting her crutch into the nearest canoe, she caught the small watercraft in her hands and pushed it down the river's bank. Her clubfoot flared with pain as it pressed into the ground. Grinding her teeth, Itala forced her body to work against its own restraints. She pushed the canoe into the water and leapt on board, taking up a paddle.

"Itala!" her father cried, splashing into the shallows and catching hold of the canoe, his massive arms keeping it from Hanna's pull. "What insanity is this? Come back to me, child, and rest yourself."

"No," Itala replied. "Let me go, Father."

"Will you embark in your own funeral canoe?" Gaher growled, tugging as though he would haul the canoe back to shore even then. "You cannot navigate these waters in the dark. The fever is upon you, and you are gone mad! Come back now."

"I must find Gaho," Itala said. Then, much to her father's surprise, she raised her paddle and swung with all the strength in her limbs. This was not much, but the paddle struck Gaher on the side of the head, startling him so that he let go and fell back into the water. By the time he stood again, dripping on the shore, his daughter was already well out into the river.

"Itala, come back!" the chieftain cried, but to no avail. The song of the morning thrush was keen in her ears, and Itala followed it.

She allowed Hanna to do most of the work, carrying her craft down its currents. She steered the nose of her canoe toward the opposite shore. When at last she heard the rapids ahead, she knew she must seek landing.

For she was not her brother, and she would not be able to survive such a mad course.

She lacked the strength to draw her canoe up onto the bank but moored it as securely as she could, knowing it would likely be pulled out into the river and lost. This did not matter. Nothing mattered except finding her brother.

She fell in the shallows but dragged herself out, her crutch trailing behind her. Shivering with cold and exhaustion, she lay in the tall grasses, afraid that she would not have the strength to go on.

The thrush sang again. In its liquid voice she believed she heard an urging. *Follow me. Follow me. Won't you follow me?*

Summoning strength she did not know she had, Itala pushed herself up and leaned heavily on her crutch. The wounds left behind by Yukka throbbed, but no more than the throbbing in her heart. Using her free hand to ward off stray branches and protect her face, Itala crashed through the forest along the river's edge, making her way slowly in pursuit of that silver voice.

Her going was slow. The night passed on over her head, and the sun appeared on the horizon. But she did not see this, for her face was to the west. She saw the crest of the bare promontory, and the stones there were stained pink and gold with morning light. Still the thrush urged her on: *Follow me. Follow me.*

Now she thought she glimpsed the bird in the branches ahead of her. A little brown body, a white, speckled breast. It led her to the promontory and into the woods growing on its lower slopes. When she stepped beneath those trees, she felt the strange sensation of stepping out of her own world.

Almost at once, a red aster bloomed at her feet. She saw it raise up its little head and unfurl its petals swiftly, like a fledgling stretching its wings. Then another bloomed beyond it. Even as she watched, a whole host of blossoms sprang up from the ground, creating a path of scarlet through the shadows and the green.

She followed it. She could not take care where she stepped, for she was clumsy, and her crutch must crush many of those small flowering faces. But they sprang up before her and behind, and she smelled the wild perfume of their hearts.

Up the hill she climbed, slowly, painfully. At last she saw the break in the trees, the bare crown of the hill before her. She saw the twisted solitary tree, but it no longer stood upright. Indeed, it was half-sunk into the soil and heavily leaning to one side.

"Itala!"

She nearly fainted, so great was the startled thrill in her heart at the sound of that voice. "Callix?" she gasped.

She found him sitting at the foot of a nearby tree. Itala hobbled to him as swiftly as she could and sank to her knees beside him, her eyes drinking in the sight of his beloved face, bright with morning light. "Are you hurt?" she cried, wondering that he did not rise to greet her. No sooner had she spoken than she saw the belt binding him tightly to the trunk of the tree.

"My arms have gone dead," Callix said, indicating the belt with a nod of his head. "When I struggle, it tightens."

Itala recognized the belt. She had seen it and its bronze fixtures around her brother's waist every day for as long as she could remember. He had worn this same belt the night he ceased to be Gaho and became the outcast, Draven.

"Where is he?" she demanded even as she worked to free Callix. He sagged in relief the moment the belt was loosed, and Itala gently massaged the blood back into his fingers, wrists, and arms. "Where is my brother?" she asked.

Callix raised sad eyes to the fallen tree. "He went down into the pit," he said. "Alone. I have not seen him return."

And Callix told Itala all that had transpired since she fell prey to the beater devil. He told how Draven found him on the exodus road with the Kahorn tribe. He told of their venture into the Wood and spoke of their meeting with Akilun.

As he spoke, he helped Itala back to her feet, and as she leaned heavily on him for support, they climbed to the crown of the promontory and stood before the dead tree. For dead it was in truth now. The pit formerly surrounding it had caved in, leaving a deep depression into which the tree had sunk. There was no sign of any stairway, of any light.

No sign of Draven.

"I would have done it," Callix said. "But your brother . . . he overpowered me. I think he knew there could be no return from such a venture. He knew he would not survive. He saved my life, Itala. Even as he did once before."

"And mine," Itala whispered, her voice so soft it scarcely made a sound. She gazed upon the twisted evil of that tree. But it was not a tree she saw.

Instead she saw her brother. Her strong, mighty brother. She saw him standing tall though his heart was fearful. She saw him descending that long stair, holding his light high. She saw it as clearly as though she had been living witness to his final efforts.

She turned to Callix then, her beloved. Seeing him alive was like seeing her own life restored to her all over again. The courage of her brother swelled in her breast.

"Callix," she said, and now her voice was strong and deep, strangely deep in her throat. "I will marry you. I will live with you on this side of the river, and I will work and serve to see your people restored. Here. In their own land, in their own country."

But the Kahorn prince frowned at this and shook his head. "That is impossible," he said. "We are too ruined. We cannot face another war with Rannul, and I would not see you endure such disaster. Your brother gave his life so that you would survive."

"No," Itala said. "My brother gave his life so that I would *live*."

The village of Rannul was all but silent, caught up in an atmosphere of anticipation. What they anticipated, none of the villagers could say. Perhaps they waited to see who would next succumb to the evil sickness. But all of them had heard the scream. All of them had seen Itala rise up from her deathbed and walk.

Somehow they knew that the dread in which they had lived since Oson's collapse was now past. But some other dread remained, something they could neither name nor understand.

All eyes turned to Gaher, who sat in the village center, his bronze ax across his knees. He too waited, though he could not have given voice to any expectation or need. He simply sat with his head bowed, sometimes muttering the same chants the warriors said before marching off to battle.

The villagers called out to each other the news of Itala's return even as her canoe was spotted on the water. Someone was with her, and rumor traveled swiftly that it was the Kahorn prince. Gaher heard but made no sign of acknowledgement. His warriors rose and held their weapons at the ready, their eyes watching their leader.

Then Itala appeared. She left her canoe on the water and her companion waiting in it with a paddle at the ready. Slow with pain and exhaustion, she progressed up from the water and along the dirt track to the village center. The sun high above shone a brilliant gold upon her hair, and her pale face, always frail, never beautiful, seemed to have acquired an ethereal glow. Quick eyes, however, could see the bruises on her neck and cheeks, could spot the increased labor in her limping stride.

Yet her steady pace did not slow as she entered the center and stood opposite her father, leaning on her crutch. Gaher, his head swollen where his daughter had struck him the night before, slowly raised his eyes to look upon Itala. The anger of his gaze was enough to cause even his bravest warriors to tremble.

"Daughter," said Gaher in the voice of a beast, "where have you been?"

"I went to seek my brother," Itala replied, making a respectful sign with her hand. "I went to seek my brother, who is dead."

The villagers turned to each other, many whispers coursing from mouth to ear at this news. But Gaher only growled, "Gaho died more than a year ago."

"And Gaheris died last night," Itala said.

True silence fell upon Rannul. All eyes fixed upon the frail girl and her mighty father. All ears rang with the sound of a name that had never been given.

Gaher said nothing. He sat still as a carved statue, his fist clenched on the hilt of his ax. Itala took a step closer, the sound of her dragging crutch loud in the ears of all listening. She said:

"Gaheris gave his life to end the evil we brought upon our own heads. For when our warriors marched upon Kahorn and spilled the blood of our brothers and sisters across the river, who had done us no harm—then we carried back with us a brutal curse. A beast. A devil. A monster that would have destroyed us one by one. There could be no fighting such a curse, for we had welcomed it into our village with feasting and celebration of bloodshed.

"But Gaheris spilled no man's blood. And when he saw our suffering, he did not say, as I did, that we deserved our fate. He went forth into the darkness. He carried with him a small light, too small, some would say! But it was enough.

"My brother Gaheris conquered the devil. My brother Gaheris gave his own life to save us."

She took another step, and her fierce gaze was like a sword thrust into the heart of her father.

"My brother Gaheris was the bravest man in all Rannul."

The chieftain did not speak. But he rose to his feet, his ax in his hand, and towered over his daughter. She faltered and did not dare to approach another step. But she drew herself up straight, standing upon both feet, without aid of her crutch. The pain of her crippled foot shot up her leg, up her spine. She ignored it.

"The courage of my brother feeds the fire of my heart," she said. "I long only to honor his name, to live a life as courageous as his. And so I have come to tell you, Father: I will marry Callix, prince of Kahorn. And I will bear his children, mingling the blood of Kahorn and Rannul forever. Even as Gaheris refused to take the blood of a man who was not his enemy, so I will join my blood with that same man."

She drew a deep breath and announced to all who stood within hearing, "The war is over."

Gaher raised his ax higher, and the gleam of its blade drew every eye to him. His warning voice rumbled deep into every heart. "If you do this thing, Itala, my child," said he, "I will kill you."

Itala let her crutch fall away behind her. She turned and strode with painful, gasping, unsupported steps to the nearest of her father's warriors. He did not resist when she reached out and took the sickle blade from his hand. Whirling about, she faced Gaher, her teeth bared in a snarl. "Do as you will, Father," she said. "My heart is set, and I will not turn aside."

Gaher approached. In three great steps, he closed in upon her, and all the villagers drew back in dread of the slaughter that must follow. But some recalled how Itala had accomplished the impossible, how she had

slain the mighty Hydrus when no other had succeeded in many generations preceding. They knew how ferocious was the heart in her breast,
and many caught their breath, waiting to see what she would do with the
weapon she bore.

None expected to see her cast the sword aside. It thudded in the dirt,
unused. And Itala lifted her clubfoot and brought it down hard in a single
step forward to meet her father's attack. She flung wide her arms,
exposing herself to his blade.

For a moment, perhaps, the villagers saw again the powerful
chieftain's son, Gaho, dropping his knife. For a moment, perhaps, they
saw him again turn to his father and say, "*It is done.*" They saw him take
upon himself the blighted name of Draven rather than spill another man's
blood.

Perhaps Gaher saw the same as they. No one could say or would
dare venture a guess. But the entire village watched how, though he drew
back his arm for the killing blow, he stopped. His ax hung suspended in
the air. Itala's life was counted in heartbeats.

Gaher gazed upon his wolf-pup daughter. The bravest heart in
Rannul.

He turned aside.

"Go," he said. "Away from here, Itala. Never set foot in Rannul
again."

As one body, the villagers released the breath they had held. The
warriors turned angry faces from their chief to the girl but made no
protest. The women and children clutched each other, and their hearts
beat with new thoughts and new ideas they had never before considered.

Itala stood frozen, her arms still outspread. Then, slowly, she
dropped them to her sides, sagged, and nearly fell. She did not fall,
however. She staggered back to her discarded crutch and retrieved it.
With the same hobbling stride she passed from the center through the

parting crowd of villagers, her people.

"Itala," said Gaher.

She paused. She did not look back but tilted her ear to catch whatever words her father might speak.

"If your sons are as brave as you," said the chief, "all Rannul will tremble with fear when the Kahorn war drums sound."

Only then did Itala look around, meeting her father's distant gaze. "If my sons are as brave as my brother Gaheris, the war drums will never sound again."

THE LEGACY OF GAHERIS

THERE," SAID AKILUN, stepping back from his work. "I do believe that is done."

The girl sat with her chin in her hands, gazing up at the carving of Draven. It was indeed complete. She saw now that he held a candle in his right hand, raised to the level of his eyes. The carefully shaped wood seemed to flicker and dance like a flame. Perhaps it was a flame indeed, captured in stillness but no less alive. And was that a reflection of the same light she saw in those wooden eyes gazing down upon her?

"Draven," she whispered. Then, "Gaheris."

"Yes. Gaheris," Akilun responded. He sat down on the floor beside her, his elbows on his knees. "You know that name, don't you?"

"I do," said she. "I did not realize Draven was the same man, the Gaheris of whom I've heard tell. And that means . . ." She turned to the Kind One, her eyes bright with tears which spilled over and streamed down her soft cheeks. "That means Itala is alive!"

"Indeed," Akilun said. "I met her soon after the story I told you ended, when I and my brother entered this world. She and her new husband told us of all that had taken place. We found Yukka defeated and the tree dead. But we also found much darkness and fear remaining in the hearts of the people. So we stayed a while to build this House. We stayed so that the light Draven first carried would shine all the brighter in this land."

"And what happened next?" the girl asked eagerly even as she wiped away her own tears. "How does the story continue?"

"Dear child," Akilun said, "what happened next is happening now. The light Draven bore into the dark places underground is still alive, still shining. It is not a light that can be buried. The hope Draven carried into this land will only blaze with greater strength over time."

"Not Draven," said the girl. "Gaheris."

Akilun bowed his head in solemn agreement. Then he said, "Our work is almost complete. Another three nights, and you will see the light shining from this hilltop."

He stood then and helped the girl to her feet. "It is late," he said. "You must return to your village now. And tell your grandmother what I said. Three more nights. Only three."

So, even as the sun began to fall from the sky, the girl hastened from the house and on down the hillside path. As she went, she believed she glimpsed red asters blooming among the twining tree roots. And in the branches over her head, was that a thrush she spied, its bright breast flashing white? Did he sing his morning song even as the dusk of evening covered the world?

Her heart was both heavy and light by turns. She wept but could not say whether they were tears of sorrow or of joy.

"Gaheris," she said to herself. "His name is Gaheris."

This truth she treasured close to her heart, even as she determined to ask one final question.

Three nights, the Kind One said. But the days in between them passed so slowly. All of Kallias village waited in eager tension. Those who worked the fields found their gazes turning up to the promontory more often than not, studying the high stone walls above them, the distant gables and sloping rooftops. Those who traversed up and down Hanna's flow turned their canoes toward the cliff looming above the river.

The girl said nothing. She did not ask her final question but held it close inside. Her grandmother had not spoken to her since her return, not even to ask if she had heard the end of the story. She had no need to ask, the girl suspected. Grandmother always knew.

Then word came down to the village, carried on the swift-flying feet of the day's water-bearer: Come to the Great House! Come, it is finished!

"It is finished," the girl whispered, in echo both of the message bearer and of another man of long years ago. Suddenly she found her grandmother beside her.

"I need your strong arm, my dear," Grandmother said. "It is a long walk up the hillside, and I am old and crippled. Will you help me?"

The girl and the old woman joined the mass of people on the road up the hill. Never before had the girl seen so many people gathered at once: all of Kallias from all over the surrounding territories, come together for this great trek. Someone near the front began to sing, and soon the song rippled down, carried by hundreds of voices. The girl heard her grandmother singing, and she blended her own small voice with the others.

It seemed to her that it was the same song the morning thrush sang, only in the words of mortals:

Beyond the Final Water falling,
The Songs of Spheres recalling,
When the sun descends behind the twilit sky
Won't you follow me?

The doors of the Great House were flung wide open as the people of Kallias approached. The enormous hall easily accommodated all who came, for it was vast and somehow seemed even bigger now that people entered within. The girl, who had already been inside, nevertheless felt overwhelmed by the beauty around her, illuminated by the torches held high in men's hands. The carvings of stone and wood. The colored tiles upon the floor. The murals, the etchings, the tapestries.

In the center was a great object wrought in silver, an enormous sphere of filigree work, large enough to contain a bonfire. A chain attached to it reached up into the rafters of the ceiling above. Off to one side, the girl glimpsed the Strong One, braced as though prepared to pull the chain and lift that silver orb up to the very heavens. But just now it rested upon the floor, and all the people of Kallias stood around it, wondering.

The moon rose. The light of it was so much brighter than the girl could have imagined. She looked up from her study of the filigree orb and watched through the open doorway as the moon appeared. Across the hall, through the opposite door, the falling sun flared equally bright, as though reaching out to the moon in glad greeting. It was far more brilliant than anything the girl had ever before seen, so beautiful that she was almost afraid.

Suddenly Akilun stood beside her, holding a candle in his hand, very like the one he had carved in Draven's fist. A light, so small compared to the glory of the sun and the moon, gleamed from its wick.

"Will you light the great lantern?" he asked her.

The girl stared, unable to speak or think. She felt her grandmother squeeze her shoulder, pushing her gently forward.

"Go on, Gahera," the old woman said. "Light the lantern."

All of Kallias watched as the girl took the candle in her hands. Akilun then led her to the orb, and she saw the wood and kindling mounded inside. Her light was so feeble; how could it possibly set such a thing ablaze?

The girl leaned forward, right into the silver lantern. She touched her candle to the kindling and watched it flicker there. Then she said, "Light up, little flame! Light up this darkness!"

The blaze caught. Akilun snatched her by the waist and pulled her back as the whole orb flared up with a white fire unlike anything the people of Kallias had ever before seen. The girl recognized it, however: It was the same light that shone in Akilun's lantern.

Akilun signaled to his brother, and Etanun the Strong One heaved upon the chain. The lantern rose up, like a celestial sphere itself. At last it was caught up into the joint glow of the sun and the moon shining through the doors. There burst over the mortals such a brilliance of color and light and, most of all, song.

The girl, still held in Akilun's arms, heard the sun and the moon singing the Songs of the Spheres. It was a language beyond anything she knew, ringing in her heart and her soul rather than her ears. She could not help but burst into song of her own, frail though it was. All of Kallias raised up its voice in anthem:

Beyond the Final Water falling,
The Songs of Spheres recalling!

The Song went on and on in bountiful echoes, reverberating throughout that massive hall.

But the girl stopped suddenly and turned to Akilun. "Where is my grandmother?" she asked, surprised that she could hear her own voice even amid that music. Perhaps it was so because she spoke in her own mortal language, which is heard with the ears.

Akilun smiled and indicated with a sweep of his hand. The girl looked where he gestured. Through the thick-gathered throng of people she saw a clear path to the far wall. The wall where Draven's statue stood.

Her grandmother stood before it, drawn up to her full height, standing straight despite the pain of her crippled foot and the bowing weight of age. She gazed into the carved face, smiling, and her smile was like the Song itself.

The girl slipped from Akilun's side and hurried to join her grandmother and the statue. Though her grandmother did not turn to her, the girl knew that she sensed her approach. She slipped her hand into the old woman's, feeling the strength there, though the grip was weak.

"Who chose my name, Grandmother?" she asked.

"I did, Gahera," her grandmother said, turning then to smile upon the girl. "I named you for my brother. And a brave name it is."

Tears fell down her face as she spoke, shining bright in the light of the sun, the moon, and the lantern high in the ceiling above.

About the Author

ANNE ELISABETH STENGL makes her home in North Carolina, where she lives with her husband, Rohan, a kindle of kitties, and one long-suffering dog. When she's not writing, she enjoys Shakespeare, opera, and tea, and practices piano, painting, and pastry baking. Her novels have been nominated for and won various literary awards, including the Christy Award and the Clive Staples Award.

To learn more about Anne Elisabeth Stengl and her books visit: www.AnneElisabethStengl.blogspot.com

COMING AUTUMN 2015

AN ALL-NEW NOVEL IN THE
TALES OF GOLDSTONE WOOD

poison crown
VOLUME I: THE SMALLMAN'S HEIR

Timeless fantasy that will keep you spellbound!

Other Exciting Books from
ROOGLEWOOD PRESS:

A dainty but deadly bodyguard, Sairu is committed to protecting her mistress, the mysterious Dream Walker. But how can she guard against enemies she can neither see nor touch? For the Dragon moves in the realm of nightmares . . .

Golden Daughter
by: Anne Elisabeth Stengl
www.GoldenDaughterNovel.blogspot.com

A timid stepsister.
A mistaken identity.
A disinherited princess.
A seething planet.
An enchanted circus.

Here are five delightful retellings to bring new life to the classic Cinderella tale!

Stories by: Elisabeth Brown, Emma Clifton Rachel Heffington, Stephanie Ricker, and Clara Diane Thompson
www.FiveGlassSlippers.blogspot.com

CPSIA information can be obtained
at www.ICGtesting.com
Printed in the USA
BVHW040721031222
653375BV00006B/126